I0642357

und Andere, Sir Arthur Conan Doyle

Stories by English Authors

Africa

und Andere, Sir Arthur Conan Doyle

Stories by English Authors
Africa

ISBN/EAN: 9783337125653

Printed in Europe, USA, Canada, Australia, Japan

Cover: Foto ©Andreas Hilbeck / pixelio.de

More available books at **www.hansebooks.com**

STORIES BY
ENGLISH AUTHORS

AFRICA

·•·

NEW YORK
CHARLES SCRIBNER'S SONS
1896

PUBLISHERS' NOTE

The stories in this volume are published by
arrangement with the authors or their pub-
lishers. Special acknowledgments are due
The American Publisher's Corporation for the
right to reprint A. Conan Doyle's story, "The
Mystery of Sasassa Valley"; to Messrs. Long-
mans, Green & Co. for Mr. Haggard's story,
"Long Odds," and to Messrs. Henry Holt &
Co. for Mr. Scully's story, "Ghamba."

CONTENTS

THE MYSTERY OF SASASSA VALLEY

BY

A. CONAN DOYLE

THE MYSTERY OF SASASSA VALLEY

BY A. CONAN DOYLE

D O I know why Tom Donahue is called " Lucky Tom "? Yes, I do ; and that is more than one in ten of those who call him so can say. I have knocked about a deal in my time, and seen some strange sights, but none stranger than the way in which Tom gained that sobriquet, and his fortune with it. For I was with him at the time. Tell it? Oh, certainly ; but it is a longish story and a very strange one ; so fill up your glass again, and light another cigar, while I try to reel it off. Yes, a very strange one ; beats some fairy stories I have heard ; but it 's true, sir, every word of it. There are men alive at Cape Colony now who 'll remember it and confirm what I say. Many a time has the tale been told round the fire in Boers' cabins from Orange State to Griqualand ; yes, and out in the bush and at the diamond-fields too.

I 'm roughish now, sir ; but I was entered at the Middle Temple once, and studied for the bar. Tom — worse luck! — was one of my fellow-students ; and a wildish time we had of it, until at last our finances ran short, and we were compelled to give up our so-called studies, and look about for some part of the world where two young fellows

with strong arms and sound constitutions might
make their mark.   In those days the tide of emigration had scarcely begun to set in toward Africa,
and so we thought our best chance would be down
at Cape Colony.   Well,—to make a long story short,
—we set sail, and were deposited in Cape Town
with less than five pounds in our pockets; and
there we parted.   We each tried our hands at
many things, and had ups and downs; but when,
at the end of three years, chance led each of us
up-country and we met again, we were, I regret to
say, in almost as bad a plight as when we started.

Well, this was not much of a commencement;
and very disheartened we were, so disheartened
that Tom spoke of going back to England and
getting a clerkship.   For you see we did n't know
that we had played out all our small cards, and
that the trumps were going to turn up.   No; we
thought our "hands" were bad all through.   It
was a very lonely part of the country that we were
in, inhabited by a few scattered farmers, whose
houses were stockaded and fenced in to defend
them against the Kaffirs.   Tom Donahue and I
had a little hut right out in the bush; but we were
known to possess nothing, and to be handy with
our revolvers, so we had little to fear.   There we
waited, doing odd jobs, and hoping that something
would turn up.   Well, after we had been there
about a month something did turn up upon a certain night, something which was the making of
both of us; and it 's about that night, sir, that I 'm

going to tell you. I remember it well. The wind
was howling past our cabin, and the rain threatened to burst in our rude window. We had a great
wood fire crackling and sputtering on the hearth,
by which I was sitting mending a whip, while Tom
was lying in his bunk groaning disconsolately at the
chance which had led him to such a place.

"Cheer up, Tom—cheer up," said I. "No
man ever knows what may be awaiting him."

"Ill luck, ill luck, Jack," he answered. "I always was an unlucky dog. Here have I been
three years in this abominable country; and I see
lads fresh from England jingling the money in
their pockets, while I am as poor as when I
landed. Ah, Jack, if you want to keep your head
above water, old friend, you must try your fortune
away from me."

"Nonsense, Tom; you 're down in your luck
to-night. But hark! Here 's some one coming
outside. Dick Wharton, by the tread; he 'll rouse
you, if any man can."

Even as I spoke the door was flung open, and
honest Dick Wharton, with the water pouring
from him, stepped in, his hearty red face looming
through the haze like a harvest-moon. He shook
himself, and after greeting us sat down by the fire
to warm himself.

"Where away, Dick, on such a night as this?"
said I. "You 'll find the rheumatism a worse foe
than the Kaffirs, unless you keep more regular
hours."

Dick was looking unusually serious, almost
frightened, one would say, if one did not know
the man.   "Had to go," he replied—"had to go.
One of Madison's cattle was seen straying down
Sasassa Valley, and of course none of our blacks
would go down *that* valley at night; and if we
had waited till morning, the brute would have
been in Kaffirland."

"Why would n't they go down Sasassa Valley
at night?" asked Tom.

"Kaffirs, I suppose," said I.

"Ghosts," said Dick.

We both laughed.

"I suppose they did n't give such a matter-of-
fact fellow as you a sight of their charms?" said
Tom, from the bunk.

"Yes," said Dick, seriously, "yes; I saw what
the niggers talk about; and I promise you, lads, I
don't want ever to see it again."

Tom sat up in his bed.   "Nonsense, Dick;
you 're joking, man!   Come, tell us all about it;
the legend first, and your own experience afterward.   Pass him over the bottle, Jack."

"Well, as to the legend," began Dick.   "It
seems that the niggers have had it handed down
to them that that Sasassa Valley is haunted by a
frightful fiend.   Hunters and wanderers passing
down the defile have seen its glowing eyes under
the shadows of the cliff; and the story goes that
whoever has chanced to encounter that baleful
glare has had his after-life blighted by the malig-

nant power of this creature. Whether that be true or not," continued Dick, ruefully, " I may have an opportunity of judging for myself."

" Go on, Dick—go on," cried Tom. " Let 's hear about what you saw."

" Well, I was groping down the valley, looking for that cow of Madison's, and I had, I suppose, got half-way down, where a black craggy cliff juts into the ravine on the right, when I halted to have a pull at my flask. I had my eye fixed at the time upon the projecting cliff I have mentioned, and noticed nothing unusual about it. I then put up my flask and took a step or two forward, when in a moment there burst, apparently from the base of the rock, about eight feet from the ground and a hundred yards from me, a strange, lurid glare, flickering and oscillating, gradually dying away and then reappearing again. No, no; I 've seen many a glow-worm and firefly—nothing of that sort. There it was, burning away, and I suppose I gazed at it, trembling in every limb, for fully ten minutes. Then I took a step forward, when instantly it vanished, vanished like a candle blown out. I stepped back again ; but it was some time before I could find the exact spot and position from which it was visible. At last, there it was, the weird reddish light, flickering away as before. Then I screwed up my courage, and made for the rock ; but the ground was so uneven that it was impossible to steer straight ; and though I walked along the whole base of the cliff, I could see nothing. Then I made tracks for home; and I can tell you, boys, that, until you remarked it, I never knew it was raining, the whole way along. But hollo! what 's the matter with Tom? "

What indeed? Tom was now sitting with his legs over the side of the bunk, and his whole face betraying excitement so intense as to be almost painful. " The fiend would have two eyes. How many lights did you see, Dick? Speak out!"

" Only one."

" Hurrah!" cried Tom, " that 's better." Where-upon he kicked the blankets into the middle of the room, and began pacing up and down with long, feverish strides. Suddenly he stopped opposite Dick, and laid his hand upon his shoulder. " I say, Dick, could we get to Sasassa Valley before sunrise? "

" Scarcely," said Dick.

" Well, look here; we are old friends, Dick Wharton, you and I. Now don't you tell any other man what you have told us, for a week. You 'll promise that, won't you? "

I could see by the look on Dick's face as he ac-quiesced that he considered poor Tom to be mad; and indeed I was myself completely mystified by his conduct. I had, however, seen so many proofs of my friend's good sense and quickness of appre-hension that I thought it quite possible that Wharton's story had had a meaning in his eyes which I was too obtuse to take in.

All night Tom Donahue was greatly excited,

and when Wharton left he begged him to remember his promise, and also elicited from him a description of the exact spot at which he had seen the
apparition, as well as the hour at which it appeared.
After his departure, which must have been about
four in the morning, I turned into my bunk and
watched Tom sitting by the fire splicing two sticks
together, until I fell asleep.   I suppose I must
have slept about two hours; but when I awoke
Tom was still sitting working away in almost the
same position.   He had fixed the one stick across
the top of the other so as to form a rough T, and
was now busy in fitting a smaller stick into the
angle between them, by manipulating which, the
cross one could be either cocked up or depressed
to any extent.   He had cut notches, too, in the
perpendicular stick, so that, by the aid of the small
prop, the cross one could be kept in any position
for an indefinite time.

"Look here, Jack!" he cried, when he saw
that I was awake.   "Come and give me your
opinion.   Suppose I put this cross-stick pointing
straight at a thing, and arranged this small one so
as to keep it so, and left it, I could find that thing
again if I wanted it—don't you think I could,
Jack—don't you think so?" he continued, nervously, clutching me by the arm.

"Well," I answered, "it would depend on how
far off the thing was, and how accurately it was
pointed.   If it were any distance, I 'd cut sights
on your cross-stick; then a string tied to the end

of it, and held in a plumb-line forward, would lead
you pretty near what you wanted. But surely,
Tom, you don't intend to localise the ghost in that
way?"

"You'll see to-night, old friend—you'll see to-
night. I'll carry this to the Sasassa Valley. You
get the loan of Madison's crowbar, and come with
me; but mind you tell no man where you are
going, or what you want it for."

All day Tom was walking up and down the
room, or working hard at the apparatus. His
eyes were glistening, his cheeks hectic, and he had
all the symptoms of high fever. "Heaven grant
that Dick's diagnosis be not correct!" I thought,
as I returned with the crowbar; and yet, as evening drew near, I found myself imperceptibly shar-
ing the excitement.

About six o'clock Tom sprang to his feet and
seized his sticks. "I can stand it no longer,
Jack," he cried; "up with your crowbar, and hey
for Sasassa Valley! To-night's work, my lad, will
either make us or mar us! Take your six-shooter,
in case we meet the Kaffirs. I dare n't take mine,
Jack," he continued, putting his hands upon my
shoulders—"I dare n't take mine; for if my ill
luck sticks to me to-night, I don't know what I
might not do with it."

Well, having filled our pockets with provisions,
we set out, and, as we took our wearisome way toward the Sasassa Valley, I frequently attempted to
elicit from my companion some clue as to his in-

tentions.   But his only answer was: "Let us hurry
on, Jack.   Who knows how many have heard of
Wharton's adventure by this time!   Let us hurry
on, or we may not be first in the field!"

Well, sir, we struggled on through the hills for
a matter of ten miles; till at last, after descending
a crag, we saw opening out in front of us a ravine
so sombre and dark that it might have been the
gate of Hades itself; cliffs many hundred feet
shut in on every side the gloomy boulder-studded
passage which led through the haunted defile into
Kaffirland.   The moon, rising above the crags,
threw into strong relief the rough, irregular pin-
nacles of rock by which they were topped, while
all below was dark as Erebus.

"The Sasassa Valley?" said I.

"Yes," said Tom.

I looked at him.   He was calm now; the flush
and feverishness had passed away; his actions were
deliberate and slow.   Yet there was a certain rigid-
ity in his face and glitter in his eye which showed
that a crisis had come.

We entered the pass, stumbling along amid the
great boulders.   Suddenly I heard a short, quick
exclamation from Tom.   "That's the crag!" he
cried, pointing to a great mass looming before us
in the darkness.   "Now, Jack, for any favour use
your eyes!   We're about a hundred yards from
that cliff, I take it; so you move slowly toward
one side and I'll do the same toward the other.
When you see anything, stop and call out.   Don't

take more than twelve inches in a step, and keep
your eye fixed on the cliff about eight feet from the
ground.   Are you ready? "

"Yes."   I was even more excited than Tom by
this time.   What his intention or object was I
could not conjecture, beyond that he wanted to
examine by daylight the part of the cliff from which
the light came.   Yet the influence of the romantic
situation and my companion's suppressed excitement was so great that I could feel the blood
coursing through my veins and count the pulses
throbbing at my temples.

"Start!" cried Tom; and we moved off, he to
the right, I to the left, each with our eyes fixed intently on the base of the crag.   I had moved perhaps twenty feet, when in a moment it burst upon
me.   Through the growing darkness there shone a
small, ruddy, glowing point, the light from which
waned and increased, flickered and oscillated, each
change producing a more weird effect than the
last.   The old Kaffir superstition came into my
mind, and I felt a cold shudder pass over me.   In
my excitement I stepped a pace backward, when
instantly the light went out, leaving utter darkness
in its place; but when I advanced again, there was
the ruddy glare glowing from the base of the cliff.
"Tom, Tom!" I cried.

"Ay, ay!" I heard him exclaim, as he hurried
over toward me.

"There it is—there, up against the cliff!"

Tom was at my elbow.   "I see nothing," said he.

"Why, there, there, man, in front of you!" I stepped to the right as I spoke, when the light instantly vanished from my eyes.

But from Tom's ejaculations of delight it was clear that from my former position it was visible to him also. "Jack," he cried, as he turned and wrung my hand—"Jack, you and I can never complain of our luck again. Now heap up a few stones where we are standing. That 's right. Now we must fix my sign-post firmly in at the top. There! It would take a strong wind to blow that down; and we only need it to hold out till morning. O Jack, my boy, to think that only yesterday we were talking of becoming clerks, and you saying that no man knew what was awaiting him, too! By Jove, Jack, it would make a good story!"

By this time we had firmly fixed the perpendicular stick in between two large stones; and Tom bent down and peered along the horizontal one. For fully a quarter of an hour he was alternately raising and depressing it, until at last, with a sigh of satisfaction, he fixed the prop into the angle, and stood up. "Look along, Jack," he said. "You have as straight an eye to take a sight as any man I know of."

I looked along. There beyond the farther sight was the ruddy, scintillating speck, apparently at the end of the stick itself, so accurately had it been adjusted.

"And now, my boy," said Tom, "let 's have some supper and a sleep. There 's nothing more to be done to-night; but we 'll need all our wits and strength to-morrow. Get some sticks and kindle a fire here, and then we 'll be able to keep an eye on our signal-post, and see that nothing happens to it during the night."

Well, sir, we kindled a fire, and had supper with the Sasassa demon's eye rolling and glowing in front of us the whole night through. Not always in the same place, though; for after supper, when I glanced along the sights to have another look at it, it was nowhere to be seen. The information did not, however, seem to disturb Tom in any way. He merely remarked, "It 's the moon, not the thing, that has shifted;" and coiling himself up, went to sleep.

By early dawn we were both up, and gazing along our pointer at the cliff; but we could make out nothing save the one dead, monotonous, slaty surface, rougher perhaps at the part we were examining than elsewhere, but otherwise presenting nothing remarkable.

"Now for your idea, Jack!" said Tom Donahue, unwinding a long thin cord from round his waist. "You fasten it, and guide me while I take the other end." So saying, he walked off to the base of the cliff, holding one end of the cord, while I drew the other taut, and wound it round the middle of the horizontal stick, passing it through the sight at the end. By this means I could direct Tom to the right or left, until we had our string stretching from the point of attachment, through the sight, and on to the rock, which it struck about eight feet from the ground. Tom drew a chalk circle of about three feet diameter round the spot, and then called to me to come and join him. "We 've managed this business together, Jack," he said, "and we 'll find what we are to find, together." The circle he had drawn embraced a part of the rock smoother than the rest, save that about the centre there were a few rough protuberances or knobs. One of these Tom pointed to with a cry of delight. It was a roughish, brownish mass about the size of a man's closed fist, and looking like a bit of dirty glass let into the wall of the cliff. "That 's it!" he cried— "that 's it!"

"That 's what?"

"Why, man, *a diamond*, and such a one as there is n't a monarch in Europe but would envy Tom Donahue the possession of. Up with your crowbar, and we 'll soon exorcise the demon of Sasassa Valley!"

I was so astounded that for a moment I stood speechless with surprise, gazing at the treasure which had so unexpectedly fallen into our hands.

"Here, hand me the crowbar," said Tom. "Now, by using this little round knob which projects from the cliff here as a fulcrum, we may be able to lever it off. Yes; there it goes. I never thought it could have come so easily. Now, Jack, the sooner we get back to our hut and then down to Cape Town, the better."

We wrapped up our treasure, and made our way across the hills toward home. On the way, Tom told me how, while a law student in the Middle Temple, he had come upon a dusty pamphlet in the library, by one Jans van Hounym, which told of an experience very similar to ours, which had befallen that worthy Dutchman in the latter part of the seventeenth century, and which resulted in the discovery of a luminous diamond. This tale it was which had come into Tom's head as he listened to honest Dick Wharton's ghost-story, while the means which he had adopted to verify his supposition sprang from his own fertile Irish brain.

"We 'll take it down to Cape Town," continued Tom, " and if we can't dispose of it with advantage there, it will be worth our while to ship for London with it. Let us go along to Madison's first, though ; he knows something of these things, and can perhaps give us some idea of what we may consider a fair price for our treasure."

We turned off from the track accordingly, before reaching our hut, and kept along the narrow path leading to Madison's farm. He was at lunch when we entered; and in a minute we were seated at each side of him, enjoying South African hospitality.

"Well," he said, after the servants were gone, " what 's in the wind now? I see you have something to say to me. What is it? "

Tom produced his packet, and solemnly untied

the handkerchiefs which enveloped it. "There!" he said, putting his crystal on the table; "what would you say was a fair price for that?"

Madison took it up and examined it critically. "Well," he said, laying it down again, "in its crude state about twelve shillings per ton."

"Twelve shillings!" cried Tom, starting to his feet. "Don't you see what it is?"

"Rock-salt!"

"Rock-salt be d—d! a diamond."

"Taste it!" said Madison.

Tom put it to his lips, dashed it down with a dreadful exclamation, and rushed out of the room.

I felt sad and disappointed enough myself; but presently, remembering what Tom had said about the pistol, I, too, left the house, and made for the hut, leaving Madison open-mouthed with astonishment. When I got in, I found Tom lying in his bunk with his face to the wall, too dispirited apparently to answer my consolations. Anathematising Dick and Madison, the Sasassa demon, and everything else, I strolled out of the hut, and refreshed myself with a pipe after our wearisome adventure. I was about fifty yards from the hut, when I heard issuing from it the sound which of all others I least expected to hear. Had it been a groan or an oath, I should have taken it as a matter of course; but the sound which caused me to stop and take the pipe out of my mouth was a hearty roar of laughter! Next moment Tom himself emerged from the

door, his whole face radiant with delight. " Game
for another ten-mile walk, old fellow? "

" What! for another lump of rock-salt, at twelve
shillings a ton? "

" ' No more of that, Hal, an you love me,' "
grinned Tom. " Now look here, Jack. What
blessed fools we are to be so floored by a trifle!
Just sit on this stump for five minutes, and I 'll
make it as clear as daylight. You 've seen many
a lump of rock-salt stuck in a crag, and so have
I, though we did make such a mull of this one.
Now, Jack, did any of the pieces you have ever
seen shine in the darkness brighter than any firefly? "

" Well, I can't say they ever did."

" I 'd venture to prophesy that if we waited
until night, which we won't do, we would see that
light still glimmering among the rocks. Therefore,
Jack, when we took away this worthless salt, we
took the wrong crystal. It is no very strange thing
in these hills that a piece of rock-salt should be
lying within a foot of a diamond. It caught our
eyes, and we were excited, and so we made fools
of ourselves, and *left the real stone behind.* Depend upon it, Jack, the Sasassa gem is lying within
that magic circle of chalk upon the face of yonder
cliff. Come, old fellow, light your pipe and stow
your revolver, and we 'll be off before that fellow
Madison has time to put two and two together."

I don't know that I was very sanguine this time.
I had begun, in fact, to look upon the diamond as

a most unmitigated nuisance. However, rather than throw a damper on Tom's expectations, I announced myself eager to start. What a walk it was! Tom was always a good mountaineer, but his excitement seemed to lend him wings that day, while I scrambled along after him as best I could.

When we got within half a mile he broke into the " double," and never pulled up until he reached the round white circle upon the cliff. Poor old Tom! when I came up, his mood had changed, and he was standing with his hands in his pockets, gazing vacantly before him with a rueful countenance.

" Look! " he said, " look! " and he pointed at the cliff. Not a sign of anything in the least resembling a diamond there. The circle included nothing but flat slate-coloured stone, with one large hole, where we had extracted the rock-salt, and one or two smaller depressions. No sign of the gem.

" I 've been over every inch of it," said poor Tom. " It 's not there. Some one has been here and noticed the chalk, and taken it. Come home, Jack ; I feel sick and tired. Oh, had any man ever luck like mine! "

I turned to go, but took one last look at the cliff first. Tom was already ten paces off.

" Hollo! " I cried, " don't you see any change in that circle since yesterday? "

" What d' ye mean? " said Tom.

"Don't you miss a thing that was there before?"

"The rock-salt?" said Tom.

"No; but the little round knob that we used
for a fulcrum. I suppose we must have wrenched
it off in using the lever. Let's have a look at
what it's made of."

Accordingly, at the foot of the cliff we searched
about among the loose stones.

"Here you are, Jack! We've done it at last!
We're made men!"

I turned round, and there was Tom radiant
with delight, and with a little corner of black rock
in his hand. At first sight it seemed to be merely
a chip from the cliff; but near the base there was
projecting from it an object which Tom was now
exultingly pointing out. It looked at first something like a glass eye; but there was a depth and
brilliancy about it such as glass never exhibited.
There was no mistake this time; we had certainly
got possession of a jewel of great value; and with
light hearts we turned from the valley, bearing
away with us the "fiend" which had so long
reigned there.

There, sir; I've spun my story out too long,
and tired you perhaps. You see, when I get talking of those rough old days, I kind of see the little
cabin again, and the brook beside it, and the bush
around, and seem to hear Tom's honest voice once
more. There's little for me to say now. We
prospered on the gem. Tom Donahue, as you

know, has set up here, and is well known about town. I have done well, farming and ostrich-raising in Africa. We set old Dick Wharton up in business, and he is one of our nearest neighbours. If you should ever be coming up our way, sir, you 'll not forget to ask for Jack Turnbull—Jack Turnbull of Sasassa Farm.

LONG ODDS

BY

H. RIDER HAGGARD

LONG ODDS

BY H. RIDER HAGGARD

THE story which is narrated in the following
pages came to me from the lips of my old
friend Allan Quatermain, or Hunter Quatermain,
as we used to call him in South Africa. He told
it to me one evening when I was stopping with
him at the place he bought in Yorkshire. Shortly
after that, the death of his only son so unsettled
him that he immediately left England, accompanied by two companions who were old fellow-
voyagers of his, Sir Henry Curtis and Captain
Good, and has now utterly vanished into the dark
heart of Africa. He is persuaded that a white
people, of which he has heard rumours all his life,
exists somewhere on the highlands in the vast, still
unexplored interior, and his great ambition is to
find them before he dies. This is the wild quest
upon which he and his companions have departed,
and from which I shrewdly suspect they never will
return. One letter only have I received from the
old gentleman, dated from a mission station high
up the Tana, a river on the east coast, about three
hundred miles north of Zanzibar; in it he says they
have gone through many hardships and adven-

tures, but are alive and well, and have found
traces which go far toward making him hope that
the results of their wild quest may be a " magnificent and unexampled discovery." I greatly fear,
however, that all he has discovered is death; for
this letter came a long while ago, and nobody has
heard a single word of the party since. They have
totally vanished.

It was on the last evening of my stay at his
house that he told the ensuing story to me and
Captain Good, who was dining with him. He
had eaten his dinner and drunk two or three
glasses of old port, just to help Good and myself
to the end of the second bottle. It was an unusual thing for him to do, for he was a most ab-
stemious man, having conceived, as he used to say,
a great horror of drink from observing its effects
upon the class of men—hunters, transport-riders,
and others—among whom he had passed so
many years of his life. Consequently the good
wine took more effect on him than it would have
done on most men, sending a little flush into his
wrinkled cheeks, and making him talk more freely
than usual.

Dear old man! I can see him now, as he went
limping up and down the vestibule, with his gray
hair sticking up in scrubbing-brush fashion, his
shrivelled yellow face, and his large dark eyes, that
were as keen as any hawk's and yet soft as a
buck's. The whole room was hung with trophies
of his numerous hunting expeditions, and he had

some story about every one of them, if only you could get him to tell them. Generally he would not, for he was not very fond of narrating his own adventures, but to-night the port wine made him more communicative.

"Ah, you brute!" he said, stopping beneath an unusually large skull of a lion, which was fixed just over the mantelpiece, beneath a long row of guns, its jaws distended to their utmost width. "Ah, you brute! you have given me a lot of trouble for the last dozen years, and will, I suppose, to my dying day."

"Tell us the yarn, Quatermain," said Good. "You have often promised to tell me, and you never have."

"You had better not ask me to," he answered, "for it is a longish one."

"All right," I said, "the evening is young and there is some more port."

Thus adjured, he filled his pipe from a jar of coarse-cut Boer tobacco that was always standing on the mantelpiece, and, still walking up and down the room, began :

"It was, I think, in the March of '69 that I was up in Sikukuni's country. It was just after old Sequati's time, and Sikukuni had got into power— I forget how. Anyway, I was there. I had heard that the Bapedi people had got down an enormous quantity of ivory from the interior, and so I started with a waggon-load of goods, and came straight away from Middelburg to try and trade some of it. It was a risky thing to go into the country so early, on account of the fever; but I knew that there were one or two others after that lot of ivory, so I determined to have a try for it, and take my chance of fever. I had got so tough from continual knocking about that I did not set it down at much. Well, I got on all right for a while. It is a wonderfully beautiful piece of bush veldt, with great ranges of mountains running through it, and round granite koppies starting up here and there, looking out like sentinels over the rolling waste of bush. But it is very hot,—hot as a stew-pan,—and when I was there that March, which, of course, is autumn in that part of Africa, the whole place reeked of fever. Every morning, as I trekked along down by the Oliphant River, I used to creep out of the waggon at dawn and look out. But there was no river to be seen—only a long line of billows of what looked like the finest cotton-wool tossed up lightly with a pitchfork. It was the fever-mist. Out from among the scrub, too, came little spirals of vapour, as though there were hundreds of tiny fires alight in it—reek rising from thousands of tons of rotting vegetation. It was a beautiful place, but the beauty was the beauty of death ; and all those lines and blots of vapour wrote one great word across the surface of the country, and that word was 'fever.'

"It was a dreadful year of illness that. I came, I remember, to one little kraal of knobnoses, and went up to it to see if I could get some *maas* (curdled buttermilk) and a few mealies. As I got near I was struck with the silence of the place. No children began to chatter, and no dogs barked. Nor could I see any native sheep or cattle. The place, though it had evidently been recently inhabited, was as still as the bush round it, and some guinea-fowl got up out of the prickly-pear bushes right at the kraal gate. I remember that I hesitated a little before going in, there was such an air of desolation about the spot. Nature never looks desolate when man has not yet laid his hand upon her breast; she is only lovely. But when man has been, and has passed away, then she looks desolate.

"Well, I passed into the kraal, and went up to the principal hut. In front of the hut was something with an old sheepskin *kaross* [rug] thrown over it. I stooped down and drew off the rug, and then shrank back amazed, for under it was the body of a young woman recently dead. For a moment I thought of turning back, but my curiosity overcame me; so, going past the woman, I went down on my hands and knees and crept into the hut. It was so dark that I could not see anything, though I could smell a great deal; so I lit a match. It was a 'tandstickor' match and burned slowly and dimly, and as the light gradually increased I made out what I thought was a lot of people, men, women, and children, fast asleep. Presently it burned up brightly, and I saw that they too, five of them altogether, were quite dead.

One was a baby.   I dropped the match in a hurry,
and was making my way out of the hut as hard as
I could go, when I caught sight of two bright eyes
staring out of a corner.   Thinking it was a wild-
cat, or some such animal, I redoubled my haste,
when suddenly a voice near the eyes began first to
mutter, and then to send up a succession of awful
yells.   Hastily I lit another match, and perceived
that the eyes belonged to an old woman, wrapped
up in a greasy leather garment.   Taking her by
the arm, I dragged her out, for she could not, or
would not, come by herself, and the stench was
overpowering me.   Such a sight as she was—a
bag of bones, covered over with black, shrivelled
parchment.   The only white thing about her was
her wool, and she seemed to be pretty well dead
except for her eyes and her voice.   She thought
that I was a devil come to take her, and that was
why she yelled so.   Well, I got her down to the
waggon, and gave her a ' tot ' of Cape smoke, and
then, as soon as it was ready, poured about a pint
of beef-tea down her throat, made from the flesh
of a blue vilder-beeste I had killed the day before,
and after that she brightened up wonderfully.   She
could talk Zulu,—indeed, it turned out that she
had run away from Zululand in T'Chaka's time,—
and she told me that all the people that I had seen
had died of fever.   When they had died, the other
inhabitants of the kraal had taken the cattle and
gone away, leaving the poor old woman, who was
helpless from age and infirmity, to perish of star-

vation or disease, as the case might be. She had been sitting there for three days among the bodies when I found her. I took her on to the next kraal, and gave the head man a blanket to look after her, promising him another if I found her well when I came back. I remember that he was much astonished at my parting with two blankets for the sake of such a worthless old creature. ' Why did I not leave her in the bush?' he asked. Those people carry the doctrine of the survival of the fittest to its extreme, you see.

" It was the night after I had got rid of the old woman that I made my first acquaintance with my friend yonder," and he nodded toward the skull that seemed to be grinning down at us in the shadow of the wide mantel-shelf. " I had trekked from dawn till eleven o'clock,—a long trek,—but I wanted to get on; and then had the oxen turned out to graze, sending the voorlooper to look after them, meaning to inspan again about six o'clock, and trek with the moon till ten. Then I got into the waggon and had a good sleep till half-past two or so in the afternoon, when I got up and cooked some meat, and had my dinner, washing it down with a pannikin of black coffee; for it was difficult to get preserved milk in those days. Just as I had finished, and the driver, a man called Tom, was washing up the things, in comes the young scoundrel of a voorlooper, driving one ox before him.

" ' Where are the other oxen?' I asked.

"'Koos!' he said, 'koos! [chief] the other oxen have gone away. I turned my back for a minute, and when I looked round again they were all gone except Kaptein, here, who was rubbing his back against a tree.'

"'You mean that you have been asleep, and let them stray, you villain. I will rub your back against a stick,' I answered, feeling very angry, for it was not a pleasant prospect to be stuck up in that fever-trap for a week or so while we were hunting for the oxen. 'Off you go, and you too, Tom, and mind you don't come back till you have found them. They have trekked back along the Middelburg road, and are a dozen miles off by now, I'll be bound. Now, no words; go, both of you.'

"Tom, the driver, swore and caught the lad a hearty kick, which he richly deserved, and then, having tied old Kaptein up to the disselboom with a riem, they got their assegais and sticks, and started. I would have gone too, only I knew that somebody must look after the waggon, and I did not like to leave either of the boys with it at night. I was in a very bad temper, indeed, although I was pretty well used to these sort of occurrences, and soothed myself by taking a rifle and going to kill something. For a couple of hours I poked about without seeing anything that I could get a shot at, but at last, just as I was again within seventy yards of the waggon, I put up an old Impala ram from behind a mimosa-thorn. He ran straight for the

waggon, and it was not till he was passing within
a few feet of it that I could get a decent shot at
him. Then I pulled, and caught him half-way
down the spine; over he went, dead as a door-
nail, and a pretty shot it was, though I ought not
to say it. This little incident put me into rather
a better temper, especially as the buck had rolled
over right against the after part of the waggon, so
I had only to gut him, fix a riem round his legs,
and haul him up. By the time I had done this
the sun was down, and the full moon was up, and
a beautiful moon it was. And then there came
down that wonderful hush that sometimes falls
over the African bush in the early hours of the
night. No beast was moving, and no bird called.
Not a breath of air stirred the quiet trees, and the
shadows did not even quiver; they only grew. It
was very oppressive and very lonely, for there was
not a sign of the cattle or the boys. I was quite
thankful for the society of old Kaptein, who was
lying down contentedly against the disselboom,
chewing the cud with a good conscience.

" Presently, however, Kaptein began to get restless. First he snorted, then he got up and snorted
again. I could not make it out, so, like a fool, I
got down off the waggon-box to have a look round,
thinking it might be the lost oxen coming.

" Next instant I regretted it, for all of a sudden
I heard an awful roar and saw something yellow
flash past me and light on poor Kaptein. Then
came a bellow of agony from the ox, and a crunch

as the lion put his teeth through the poor brute's neck, and I began to realise what had happened. My rifle was in the waggon, and my first thought was to get hold of it, and I turned and made a bolt for it. I got my foot on the wheel and flung my body forward on to the waggon, and there I stopped as if I were frozen, and no wonder, for as I was about to spring up I heard the lion behind me, and next second I felt the brute, ay, as plainly as I can feel this table. I felt him, I say, sniffing at my left leg that was hanging down.

"My word! I did feel queer; I don't think that I ever felt so queer before. I dared not move for the life of me, and the odd thing was that I seemed to lose power over my leg, which had an insane sort of inclination to kick out of its own mere motion—just as hysterical people want to laugh when they ought to be particularly solemn. Well, the lion sniffed and sniffed, beginning at my ankle and slowly nosing away up to my thigh. I thought that he was going to get hold then, but he did not. He only growled softly, and went back to the ox. Shifting my head a little I got a full view of him. He was the biggest lion I ever saw,—and I have seen a great many,—and he had a most tremendous black mane. What his teeth were like you can see—look there, pretty big ones, ain't they? Altogether he was a magnificent animal, and, as I lay there sprawling on the fore tongue of the waggon, it occurred to me that he would look uncommonly well in a cage. He stood there by the carcass of poor Kaptein, and deliberately disembowelled him as neatly as a butcher could have done. All this while I dared not move, for he kept lifting his head and keeping an eye on me as he licked his bloody chops. When he had cleaned Kaptein out, he opened his mouth and roared, and I am not exaggerating when I say that the sound shook the waggon. Instantly there came back an answering roar.

" ' Heavens!' I thought, ' there is his mate.'

" Hardly was the thought out of my head when I caught sight in the moonlight of the lioness bounding along through the long grass, and after her a couple of cubs about the size of mastiffs. She stopped within a few feet of my head, and stood, and waved her tail, and fixed me with her glowing yellow eyes; but just as I thought that it was all over she turned, and began to feed on Kaptein, and so did the cubs. There were the four of them within eight feet of me, growling and quarrelling, rending and tearing and crunching poor Kaptein's bones; and there I lay shaking with terror, and the cold perspiration pouring out of me, feeling like another Daniel come to judgment in a new sense of the phrase. Presently the cubs had eaten their fill, and began to get restless. One went round to the back of the waggon and pulled at the Impala buck that hung there, and the other came round my way and began the sniffing game at my leg. Indeed, he did more than that, for, my trouser being hitched up a little, he began to lick the bare skin with his rough tongue. The more he licked the more he liked it, to judge from his increased vigour and the loud purring noise he made. Then I knew that the end had come, for in another second his file-like tongue would have rasped through the skin of my leg—which was luckily pretty tough—and have got to the blood, and then there would be no chance for me. So I just lay there and thought of my sins, and prayed to the Almighty, and thought that, after all, life was a very enjoyable thing.

"And then all of a sudden I heard a crashing of bushes and the shouting and whistling of men, and there were the two boys coming back with the cattle, which they had found trekking along all together. The lions lifted their heads and listened, and then without a sound bounded off—and I fainted.

"The lions came back no more that night, and by the next morning my nerves had got pretty straight again; but I was full of wrath when I thought of all that I had gone through at the hands, or rather noses, of those four lions, and of the fate of my after-ox Kaptein. He was a splendid ox, and I was very fond of him. So wroth was I that, like a fool, I determined to go for the whole family of them. It was worthy of a greenhorn out on his first hunting-trip; but I did it nevertheless. Accordingly after breakfast, having rubbed some oil upon my leg, which was very sore from the cub's tongue, I took the driver, Tom, who did not half like the job, and having armed myself with an ordinary double No. 12 smooth-bore, the first breech-loader I ever had, I started. I took the smooth-bore because it shot a bullet very well; and my experience has been that a round ball from a smooth-bore is quite as effective against a lion as an express bullet. The lion is soft and not a difficult animal to finish if you hit him anywhere in the body. A buck takes far more killing.

" Well, I started, and the first thing I set to work to do was to try to make out whereabouts the brutes lay up for the day. About three hundred yards from the waggon was the crest of a rise covered with single mimosa-trees, dotted about in a park-like fashion, and beyond this was a stretch of open plain running down to a dry pan, or water-hole, which covered about an acre of ground, and was densely clothed with reeds, now in the sear and yellow leaf. From the farther edge of this pan the ground sloped up again to the great cleft, or nullah, which had been cut out by the action of water, and was pretty thickly sprinkled with bush, among which grew some large trees, I forget of what sort.

" It at once struck me that the dry pan would be a likely place to find my friends in, as there is nothing a lion is fonder of than lying up in reeds, through which he can see things without being seen himself. Accordingly thither I went and pro-spected. Before I had got half-way round the pan I

found the remains of a blue vilder-beeste that had
evidently been killed within the last three or four
days and partially devoured by lions; and from
other indications about I was soon assured that if
the family were not in the pan that day, they
spent a good deal of their spare time there. But
if there, the question was how to get them out; for
it was clearly impossible to think of going in after
them unless one was quite determined to commit
suicide. Now there was a strong wind blowing
from the direction of the waggon, across the reedy
pan, toward the bush-clad kloof or donga, and this
first gave me the idea of firing the reeds, which, as
I think I told you, were pretty dry. Accordingly
Tom took some matches and began starting little
fires to the left, and I did the same to the right.
But the reeds were still green at the bottom, and
we should never have got them well alight had it
not been for the wind, which got stronger and
stronger as the sun got higher, and forced the fire
into them. At last, after half an hour's trouble,
the flames got a hold, and began to spread out like
a fan, whereupon I got round to the farther side
of the pan to wait for the lions, standing well out
in the open, as we stood at the copse to-day where
you shot the woodcock. It was a rather risky
thing to do, but I used to be so sure of my shooting in those days that I did not so much mind the
risk. Scarcely had I got round when I heard the
reeds parting before the onward rush of some
animal. 'Now for it,' said I. On it came. I

could see that it was yellow, and prepared for action, when instead of a lion out bounded a beautiful rietbok which had been lying in the shelter of the pan. It must, by the way, have been a rietbok of a peculiarly confiding nature to lay itself down with the lion like the lamb of prophecy, but I suppose that the reeds were thick, and that it kept a long way off.

"Well, I let the rietbok go, and it went like the wind, and kept my eyes fixed upon the reeds. The fire was burning like a furnace now; the flames crackling and roaring as they bit into the reeds, sending spouts of fire twenty feet and more into the air, and making the hot air dance above it in a way that was perfectly dazzling. But the reeds were still half green, and created an enormous quantity of smoke, which came rolling toward me like a curtain, lying very low on account of the wind. Presently, above the crackling of the fire, I heard a startled roar, then another and another. So the lions were at home.

"I was beginning to get excited now, for, as you fellows know, there is nothing in experience to warm up your nerves like a lion at close quarters, unless it is a wounded buffalo; and I got still more so when I made out through the smoke that the lions were all moving about on the extreme edge of the reeds. Occasionally they would pop their heads out like rabbits from a burrow, and then, catching sight of me standing about fifty yards out, draw them back again. I knew that it

must be getting pretty warm behind them, and
that they could not keep the game up for long;
and I was not mistaken, for suddenly all four of
them broke cover together, the old black-maned
lion leading by a few yards. I never saw a more
splendid sight in all my hunting experience than
those four lions bounding across the veldt, over-
shadowed by the dense pall of smoke and backed
by the fiery furnace of the burning reeds.

" I reckoned that they would pass, on their road
to the bushy kloof, within about five and twenty
yards of me; so, taking a long breath, I got my
gun well on to the lion's shoulder—the black-
maned one—so as to allow for an inch or two of
motion, and catch him through the heart. I was
on, dead on, and my finger was just beginning to
tighten on the trigger, when suddenly I went blind
—a bit of reed-ash had drifted into my right eye.
I danced and rubbed, and got it more or less clear
just in time to see the tail of the last lion vanishing
round the bushes up the kloof.

"If ever a man was mad I was that man. It
was too bad; and such a shot in the open, too!
However, I was not going to be beaten, so I
just turned and marched for the kloof. Tom, the
driver, begged and implored me not to go; but
though as a general rule I never pretended to be
very brave (which I am not), I was determined
that I would either kill those lions or they should
kill me. So I told Tom that he need not come
unless he liked, but I was going; and being a

plucky fellow, a Swazi by birth, he shrugged his shoulders, muttered that I was mad or bewitched, and followed doggedly in my tracks.

"We soon got to the kloof, which was about three hundred yards in length and but sparsely wooded, and then the real fun began. There might be a lion behind every bush—there certainly were four lions somewhere; the delicate question was, where. I peeped and poked and looked in every possible direction, with my heart in my mouth, and was at last rewarded by catching a glimpse of something yellow moving behind a bush. At the same moment, from another bush opposite me out burst one of the cubs and galloped back toward the burned-out pan. I whipped round and let drive a snap-shot that tipped him head over heels, breaking his back within two inches of the root of the tail, and there he lay helpless but glaring. Tom afterward killed him with his assegai. I opened the breech of the gun and hurriedly pulled out the old case, which, to judge from what ensued, must, I suppose, have burst and left a portion of its fabric sticking to the barrel. At any rate, when I tried to get in the new case it would only enter half-way; and—would you believe it? —this was the moment that the lioness, attracted no doubt by the outcry of her cub, chose to put in an appearance. There she stood, twenty paces or so from me, lashing her tail and looking just as wicked as it is possible to conceive. Slowly I stepped backward, trying to push in the new case, and as I did so she moved on in little runs, dropping down after each run. The danger was imminent, and the case would not go in. At the moment I oddly enough thought of the cartridge-maker, whose name I will not mention, and earnestly hoped that if the lion got me some condign punishment would overtake him. It would not go in, so I tried to pull it out. It would not come out, either, and my gun was useless if I could not shut it to use the other barrel. I might as well have had no gun. Meanwhile I was walking backward, keeping my eye on the lioness, who was creeping forward on her belly without a sound, but lashing her tail and keeping her eye on me ; and in it I saw that she was coming in a few seconds more. I dashed my wrist and the palm of my hand against the brass rim of the cartridge till the blood poured from them—look, there are the scars of it to this day!"

Here Quatermain held up his right hand to the light and showed us seven or eight white cicatrices just where the wrist is set into the hand.

"But it was not of the slightest use," he went on ; "the cartridge would not move. I only hope that no other man will ever be put in such an awful position. The lioness gathered herself together, and I gave myself up for lost, when suddenly Tom shouted out from somewhere in my rear :

"'You are walking on to the wounded cub ; turn to the right.'

" I had the sense, dazed as I was, to take the hint, and slewing round at right angles, but still keeping my eyes on the lioness, I continued my backward walk.

" To my intense relief, with a low growl she straightened herself, turned, and bounded off farther up the kloof.

" 'Come on, inkoos,' said Tom; ' let 's get back to the waggon.'

" ' All right, Tom,' I answered. ' I will when I have killed those three other lions,' for by this time I was bent on shooting them as I never remember being bent on anything before or since. ' You can go if you like, or you can get up a tree.'

" He considered the position a little, and then he very wisely got up a tree. I wish that I had done the same.

" Meanwhile I had got out my knife, which had an extractor in it, and succeeded after some difficulty in hauling out the case which had so nearly been the cause of my death, and removing the obstruction in the barrel. It was very little thicker than a postage-stamp; certainly not thicker than a piece of writing-paper. This done I loaded the gun, bound my handkerchief round my wrist and hand to stanch the flowing of the blood, and started on again.

" I had noticed that the lioness went into a thick green bush, or rather cluster of bushes, growing near the water; for there was a little stream running down the kloof, about fifty yards higher

up, and for this I made. When I got there, however, I could see nothing, so I took up a big stone
and threw it into the bushes.   I believe that it hit
the other cub, for out it came with a rush, giving
me a broadside shot of which I promptly availed
myself, knocking it over dead.   Out, too, came the
lioness like a flash of light, but quick as she went
I managed to put the other bullet into her ribs, so
that she rolled right over three times like a shot
rabbit.   I instantly got two more cartridges into
the gun, and as I did so the lioness got up again
and came crawling toward me on her fore paws,
roaring and groaning, and with such an expression
of diabolical fury on her countenance as I have
not often seen.   I shot her again through the
chest, and she fell over on to her side quite dead.

"That was the first and last time that I ever killed
a brace of lions right and left, and, what is more,
I never heard of anybody else doing it.   Naturally
I was considerably pleased with myself, and, having again loaded up, went on to look for the black-
maned beauty who had killed Kaptein.   Slowly
and with the greatest care I proceeded up the
kloof, searching every bush and tuft of grass as I
went.   It was wonderfully exciting work, for I
never was sure from one moment to another but
that he would be on me.   I took comfort, however, from the reflection that a lion rarely attacks
a man,—rarely, I say; sometimes he does, as you
will see,—unless he is cornered or wounded.   I
must have been nearly an hour hunting after the

lion. Once I thought I saw something move in a clump of tambouki grass, but I could not be sure, and when I trod out the grass I could not find him.

" At last I got up to the head of the kloof, which made a cul-de-sac. It was formed of a wall of rock about fifty feet high. Down this rock trickled a little waterfall, and in front of it, some seventy feet from its face, was a great piled-up mass of boulders, in the crevices and on the top of which grew ferns and grass and stunted bushes. This mass was about twenty-five feet high. The sides of the kloof here were also very steep. Well, I got up to the top of the nullah and looked all round. No signs of the lion. Evidently I had either over-looked him farther down, or he had escaped right away. It was very vexatious; but still three lions were not a bad bag for one gun before dinner, and I was fain to be content. Accordingly I departed back again, making my way round the isolated pillar of boulders, and beginning to feel that I was pretty well done up with excitement and fatigue, and should be more so before I had skinned those three lions. When I had got, as nearly as I could judge, about eighteen yards past the pillar or mass of boulders, I turned to have an-other look round. I have a pretty sharp eye, but I could see nothing at all.

"Then, on a sudden, I saw something suffi-ciently alarming. On the top of the mass of boul-ders, opposite to me, standing out clear against the rock beyond, was the huge black-maned lion.

He had been crouching there, and now arose as though by magic. There he stood lashing his tail, just like a statue of the animal on the gateway of Northumberland House that I have seen a picture of. But he did not stand long. Before I could fire—before I could do more than get the gun to my shoulder—he sprang straight up and out from the rock, and, driven by the impetus of that one mighty bound, came hurtling through the air toward me.

"Heavens! how grand he looked, and how awful! High into the air he flew, describing a great arch. Just as he touched the highest point of his spring I fired. I did not dare to wait, for I saw that he would clear the whole space and land right upon me. Without a sight, almost without aim, I fired, as one would fire a snap-shot at a snipe. The bullet told, for I distinctly heard its thud above the rushing sound caused by the passage of the lion through the air. Next second I was swept to the ground (luckily I fell into a low, creeper-clad bush, which broke the shock), and the lion was on the top of me, and the next those great white teeth of his had met in my thigh—I heard them grate against the bone. I yelled out in agony, for I did not feel in the least benumbed and happy, like Dr. Livingstone,—whom, by the way, I knew very well,—and gave myself up for dead. But suddenly, as I did so, the lion's grip on my thigh loosened, and he stood over me, swaying to and fro, his huge mouth, from which the blood was gushing, wide opened. Then he roared, and the sound shook the rocks.

"To and fro he swung, and suddenly the great head dropped on me, knocking all the breath from my body, and he was dead. My bullet had entered in the centre of his chest and passed out on the right side of the spine about half-way down the back.

"The pain of my wound kept me from fainting, and as soon as I got my breath I managed to drag myself from under him. Thank heavens, his great teeth had not crushed my thigh-bone; but I was losing a great deal of blood, and had it not been for the timely arrival of Tom, with whose aid I got the handkerchief off my wrist and tied it round my leg, twisting it tight with a stick, I think I should have bled to death.

"Well, it was a just reward for my folly in trying to tackle a family of lions single-handed. The odds were too long. I have been lame ever since, and shall be to my dying day; in the month of March the wound always troubles me a great deal, and every three years it breaks out raw. I need scarcely add that I never traded the lot of ivory at Sikukuni's. Another man got it—a German— and made five hundred pounds out of it after paying expenses. I spent the next month on the broad of my back, and was a cripple for six months after that. And now I 've told you the yarn, so I will have a drop of hollands and go to bed."

KING BEMBA'S POINT

A WEST AFRICAN STORY

BY

J. LANDERS

KING BEMBA'S POINT

A WEST AFRICAN STORY

BY J. LANDERS

W E were for the most part a queer lot out on that desolate southwest African coast, in charge of the various trading stations that were scattered along the coast, from the Gaboon River, past the mouth of the mighty Congo, to the Portuguese city of St. Paul de Loanda. A mixture of all sorts, especially of bad sorts: broken-down clerks, men who could not succeed any-where else, sailors, youths, and some whose characters would not have borne any investigation ; and we very nearly all drank hard, and those who did n't drink hard took more than was good for them.

I don't know exactly what induced me to go out there. I was young for one thing, the country was unknown, the berth was vacant, and the conditions of it easy.

Imagine a high rocky point or headland, stretching out sideways into the sea, and at its base a small river winding into a country that was seem-

ingly a blank in regard to inhabitants or cultiva-
tion; a land continuing for miles and miles, as far
as the eye could see, one expanse of long yellow
grass, dotted here and there with groups of bastard
palms. In front of the headland rolled the lonely
South Atlantic; and, as if such conditions were
not dispiriting enough to existence upon the Point,
there was yet another feature which at times gave
the place a still more ghastly look. A long way
off the shore, the heaving surface of the ocean
began, in anything like bad weather, to break upon
the shoals of the coast. Viewed from the top of
the rock, the sea at such times looked, for at least
two miles out, as if it were scored over with lines
of white foam; but lower down, near the beach,
each roller could be distinctly seen, and each roller
had a curve of many feet, and was an enormous
mass of water that hurled itself shoreward until it
curled and broke.

When I first arrived on the Point there was, I
may say, only one house upon it, and that belonged to Messrs. Flint Brothers, of Liverpool.
It was occupied by one solitary man named Jackson; he had had an assistant, but the assistant
had died of fever, and I was sent to replace him.
Jackson was a man of fifty at least, who had
been a sailor before he had become an African
trader. His face bore testimony to the winds and
weather it had encountered, and wore habitually
a grave, if not melancholy, expression. He was
rough but kind to me, and though strict was just,

which was no common feature in an old African
hand to one who had just arrived on the coast.

He kept the factory—we called all houses on the
coast factories—as neat and clean as if it had been
a ship. He had the floor of the portion we dwelt
in holystoned every week; and numberless little
racks and shelves were fitted up all over the house.
The outside walls glittered with paint, and the yard
was swept clean every morning; and every Sunday,
at eight o'clock and sunset, the ensign was hoisted
and lowered, and an old cannon fired at the word
of command. Order and rule were with Jackson
observed from habit, and were strictly enforced by
him on all the natives employed in the factory.

Although I have said the country looked as if
uninhabited, there were numerous villages hidden
away in the long grass and brushwood, invisible at
a distance, being huts of thatch or mud, and not
so high as the grass among which they were
placed. From these villages came most of our
servants, and also the middlemen, who acted as
brokers between us, the white men, and the negroes
who brought ivory and gum and india-rubber
from the far interior for sale. Our trade was prin-
cipally in ivory, and when an unusually large number of elephants' tusks arrived upon the Point for
sale, it would be crowded with Bushmen, strange
and uncouth, and hideously ugly, and armed, and
then we would be very busy; for sometimes as
many as two hundred tusks would be brought to
us at the same time, and each of these had to be

bargained for and paid for by exchange of cotton cloths, guns, knives, powder, and a host of small wares.

For some time after my arrival our factory, along with the others on the coast belonging to Messrs. Flint Brothers, was very well supplied by them with goods for the trade; but by degrees their shipments became less frequent, and small when they did come. In spite of repeated letters we could gain no reason from the firm for this fact, nor could the other factories, and gradually we found ourselves with an empty storehouse, and nearly all our goods gone. Then followed a weary interval, during which we had nothing whatever to do, and day succeeded day through the long hot season. It was now that I began to feel that Jackson had become of late more silent and reserved with me than ever he had been. I noticed, too, that he had contracted a habit of wandering out to the extreme end of the Point, where he would sit for hours gazing upon the ocean before him. In addition to this, he grew morose and uncertain in his temper toward the natives, and sometimes he would fall asleep in the evenings on a sofa, and talk to himself at such a rate while asleep that I would grow frightened, and wake him, when he would stare about him for a little until he gathered consciousness, and then he would stagger off to bed to fall asleep again almost immediately. Also, his hands trembled much, and he began to lose flesh. All this troubled me, for his own sake as well as my own, and I resolved to ask him to see the doctor of the next mail-steamer that came. With this idea I went one day to the end of the Point, and found him in his usual attitude, seated on the long grass, looking seaward. He did not hear me approach, and when I spoke he started to his feet, and demanded fiercely why I disturbed him. I replied, as mildly as I could, for I was rather afraid of the glittering look that was in his eyes, that I wished to ask him if he did not feel ill.

He regarded me with a steady but softened glance for a little, and then said:

" My lad, I thank you for your trouble; but I want no doctor. Do you think I 'm looking ill? "

" Indeed you are," I answered, "ill and thin; and, do you know, I hear you talk to yourself in your sleep nearly every night."

" What do I say ? " he asked, eagerly.

" That I cannot tell," I replied. " It is all rambling talk; the same things over and over again, and nearly all about one person—Lucy."

" Boy! " he cried out, as if in pain, or as if something had touched him to the quick, "sit you down, and I 'll tell you why I think of her—she was my wife."

He moved nearer to the edge of the cliff, and we sat down, almost over the restless sea beneath us.

" She lives in my memory," he continued, speaking more to himself than to me, and looking far

out to the horizon, beneath which the setting sun
had begun to sink, "in spite of all I can do or
think of to make her appear base in my eyes.
For she left me to go with another man—a
scoundrel. This was how it was," he added,
quickly: "I married her, and thought her as pure
as a flower; but I could not take her to sea with
me because I was only the mate of a vessel, so I
left her among her own friends, in the village
where she was born. In a little cottage by herself
I settled her, comfortable and happy as I thought.
God! how she hung round my neck and sobbed
when I went away the first time! and yet—yet—
within a year she left me." And he stopped for
several minutes, resting his head upon his hands.
"At first I could get no trace of her," he resumed.
"Her friends knew nothing more of her than that
she had left the village suddenly. Gradually I
found out the name of the scoundrel who had se-
duced her away. He had bribed her friends so
that they were silent; but I overbribed them with
the last money that I had, and I followed him and
my wife on foot. I never found them, nor did I
ever know why she had deserted me for him. If
I had only known the reason; if I could have
been told of my fault; if she had only written to
say that she was tired of me; that I was too old,
too rough for her soft ways,—I think I could have
borne the heavy stroke the villain had dealt me
better. The end of my search was that I dropped
down in the streets of Liverpool, whither I thought

I had tracked them, and was carried to the hospital with brain-fever upon me. Two months afterward I came out cured, and the sense of my loss was deadened within me, so that I could go to sea again, which I did, before the mast, under the name of Jackson, in a bark that traded to this coast here." And the old sailor rose to his feet and turned abruptly away, leaving me sitting alone.

I saw that he did not wish to be followed, so I stayed where I was and watched the gray twilight creep over the face of the sea, and the night quickly succeed to it. Not a cloud had been in the sky all the day long, and as the darkness increased the stars came out, until the whole heavens were studded with glittering gems.

Suddenly, low down, close to the sea, a point of light flickered and disappeared, shone again for a moment, wavered and went out, only to reappear and shine steadily. "A steamer's masthead light," I thought, and ran to the house to give the news; but Jackson had already seen the light, and pronounced it to be that of a mail-steamer, and shortly we saw her side-lights, and the sound of a gun announced that she had anchored until the morning. At daybreak there she was, dipping her sides to the swell of the sea as it rolled beneath her. It was my duty to go off to her in one of the surf-boats belonging to the factory; and so I scrambled down the cliff to the little strip of smooth beach that served us for a landing-place.

When I arrived there I found that the white-
crested breakers were heavier than I had thought
they would be. However, there was the boat lying on the beach with its prow toward the waves,
and round it were the boat-boys with their loin-
cloths girded, ready to start ; so I clambered into
the stern, or rather—for the boat was shaped alike
at stem and stern—the end from which the steers-
man, or *patrao*, used his long oar. With a shout
the boys laid hold of the sides of the boat, and the
next moment it was dancing on the spent waves
next to the beach. The patrao kept its head
steady, and the boys jumped in and seized the
oars, and began pulling with a will, standing up
to their stroke. Slowly the heavy craft gathered
way, and approached a dark and unbroken roller
that hastened toward the beach. Then the patrao
shouted to the crew, and they lay on their oars, and
the wave with a roar burst right in front of the
boat, sending the spray of its crest high above our
heads.

"*Rema! rema força!*" ("Row strongly!") now
shouted the patrao, speaking Portuguese, as mostly
all African coast natives do; and the crew gave
way. The next roller we had to meet in its
strength; and save for the steady force of the
patrao's oar, I believe it would have tossed us
aside and we would have been swept under its
curving wall of water. As it was, the good boat
gave a mighty bound as it felt its force, and its

stem pitched high into the air as it slid down its broad back into the deep.

Another and yet another wave were passed, and we could now see them breaking behind us, shutting out the beach from view. Then the last roller was overcome, and there was nothing but the long heave of the deep sea to contend against. Presently we arrived at the steamer, whose side towered above us—an iron wall.

A shout came to me, pitching and lurching with the boat far below, "Come on board at once." But to come on board was only to be done by watching a chance as the boat rose on the top of a roller. Taking such a one, I seized the side-ropes, swung a moment in mid-air, and the next was on the steamer's clean white deck. Before me stood a tall man with black hair and whiskers and dark piercing eyes, who asked me if I was the agent for Flint Brothers. I answered that the agent was on shore, and that I was his assistant. Whereupon he informed me that he had been appointed by the firm to liquidate all their stations and businesses on the coast, and "he would be obliged by my getting his luggage into the boat." This was said in a peremptory sort of way, as if he had spoken to a servant; and very much against the grain I obeyed his orders.

That the man was new to the coast was evident, and my consolation was that he would be very soon sick of it and pretty well frightened before he even

got on shore, for the weather was freshening rapidly, a fact of which he appeared to take no heed.
Not so the boat-boys, who were anxious to be off.
At last we started, and I soon had my revenge. As
we drew near the shore the rollers became higher
and higher, and I perceived that my gentleman
clutched the gunwale of the boat very tightly, and
when the first wave that showed signs of breaking
overtook us, he grew very white in the face until
it had passed.

The next one or two breakers were small, much
to his relief I could see, though he said nothing.
Before he had well recovered his equanimity, however, a tremendous wave approached us somewhat
suddenly. Appalled by its threatening aspect, he
sprang from his seat and seized the arm of the
patrao, who roughly shook him off.

"My God!" he cried, "we are swamped!" and
for the moment it really looked like it; but the
patrao, with a dexterous sweep of his long oar,
turned the boat's head toward the roller. It
broke just as it reached us, and gave us the benefit
of its crest, which came in over the topsides of the
boat as it passed by, and deluged every one of us.

I laughed, although it was no laughing matter,
at the plight the liquidator was now in. He was
changed in a moment from a spruce and natty per-
sonage into a miserable and draggled being. From
every part of him the salt water was streaming, and
the curl was completely taken out of his whiskers.
He could not speak from terror, which the boat-boys

soon saw, for none are quicker than negroes to de-
tect signs of fear in those whom they are accustomed to consider superior to themselves. Familiar with the surf, and full of mischievous fun, they
began to shout and gesticulate with the settled
purpose of making matters appear worse than they
were, and of enjoying the white man's discom-
fiture,—all but the patrao, who was an old hand,
and on whom depended the safety of us all. He
kept a steady lookout seaward, and stood upright
and firm, grasping his oar with both hands. With
him it was a point of honour to bring the white
men intrusted to his care safely through the surf.

We waited for more than half an hour, bow on,
meeting each roller as it came to us; and by the
end of that time the unfortunate liquidator had
evidently given up all hope of ever reaching the
shore. Luckily, the worst was soon to pass. After
one last tremendous wave there was a lull for a few
moments, and the patrao, who had watched for
such a chance, swiftly turned the boat round, and
giving the word to the crew, they pulled lustily toward the shore. In a few minutes we were again
in safety. The boat grounded on the beach; the
oars were tossed into the sea; the crew sprang
overboard; some of them seized the new arrival; I
clambered on the back of the patrao; a crowd of
negroes, who had been waiting on the beach, laid
hold of the tow-rope of the boat, and it and we
were landed simultaneously on the dry sand.

Once on shore Mr. Bransome, for that was the

new man's name, rapidly recovered his presence
of mind and manner, and, by way of covering his
past confusion, remarked that he supposed the surf
was seldom so bad as it then was. I replied in an
offhand way, meaning to make fun of him, that
what he had passed through was nothing, and ap-
pealed to the patrao to confirm what I had said.
That negro, seeing the joke, grinned all over his
black face; and Mr. Bransome, perceiving that he
was being laughed at, snatched a good-sized stick
from a native standing near, and struck the patrao
repeatedly over the back.

In vain Sooka, for that was the patrao's name,
protested, and demanded to know what wrong
thing he had done. The agent was furious, and
showered his blows upon the black. Equally in
vain I shouted that Sooka had done well by us, and
that he, Mr. Bransome, was making an enemy of
a man who would have him now and then in his
power. At length Sooka took to his heels, and,
sure enough, when he had got a little way off, he
began to threaten vengeance for what he had received. I sympathised with him, for I knew what
a loss to his dignity it was to be beaten without
cause before his fellows, and I feared that Mr.
Bransome would indeed be sorry, sooner or later,
for what he had done.

I now suggested to him, by way of diverting his
thoughts from poor Sooka, that standing on the
beach in wet clothes was the very way to catch
the coast-fever straight off, and he instantly suf-

fered himself to be carried up to the factory.
There Jackson received him in a sort of "who on
earth are you?" manner; and Mr. Bransome, clear-
ing his throat, announced himself and his author-
ity, adding that he intended to make the factory
a point of departure to all the others on the coast;
then, very abruptly, he requested Jackson to pre-
pare quarters for him without delay.

The change that came over Jackson's face as he
learned the quality of the stranger and his requests
was great. The old salt, who had been king of his
house and of the Point for so long a time, had
evidently never even thought of the probability of
such an intrusion as was now presented to him, and
he was amazed at what he considered to be the
unwarrantable assurance of the stranger. However, he recovered himself smartly, and asked the
new man if he had any written credentials.

"Certainly," replied he, pulling out a document
all wet with salt water. "Here is a letter from
Messrs. Flint Brothers, of which, no doubt, you
will have a copy in your mail-bag."

Jackson took the letter and opened it, and
seemed to read it slowly to himself. All at once
he started, looked at the new agent, advanced a
step or two toward him, muttering, "Bransome,
Bransome," then stopped and asked him in a
strange constrained voice, "Is *your* name Bransome?"

"Yes," replied the latter, astonished at the old
man's question.

"I knew a Bransome once," said Jackson, steadily, "and he was a scoundrel."

For a moment the two men looked at each other—Jackson with a gleam of hatred in his eyes, while Bransome had a curiously frightened expression on his face, which blanched slightly. But he quickly resumed his composure and peremptory way, and said, "Show me a room; I must get these wet things off me."

As, however, he addressed himself this time to me rather than to Jackson,—who, indeed, regarded him no longer, but stood with the letter loose in his hand, looking at the floor of the room, as if in deep meditation,—I showed him into my own room, where I ordered his trunks to be brought. These, of course, were wet; but he found some things in the middle of them that were not more than slightly damp, and with the help of a pair of old canvas trousers of mine he managed to make his appearance at dinner-time.

Jackson was not at the meal. He had left the house shortly after his interview with the new agent, and had, I fancied, gone on one of his solitary rambles. At any rate he did not return until late that night.

I thought Mr. Bransome seemed to be somewhat relieved when he saw that the old man was not coming; and he became more affable than I had expected him to be, and relinquished his arrogant style altogether when he began to question me about Jackson—who he was? what had he been? how long he had lived on the coast? To all which questions I returned cautious answers, remembering that I was under a promise to the old man not to repeat his story.

By the next morning, to my surprise, Jackson appeared to have become reconciled to the fact that he had been superseded by a man who knew nothing of the coast, and of his own accord he · offered to tell Mr. Bransome the clues to the letter-locks on the doors of the various store-rooms; for we on the coast used none but letter-locks, which are locks that do not require a key to open them. But Mr. Bransome expressed, most politely, a wish that Jackson should consider himself still in charge of the factory, at any rate until the whole estate of the unfortunate Flint Brothers could be wound up; and he trusted that his presence would make no difference to him.

This was a change, on the part of both men, from the manners of the previous day; and yet I could not help thinking that each but ill concealed his aversion to the other.

Months now slipped away, and Mr. Bransome was occupied in going up and down the coast in a little steamer, shutting up factory after factory, transferring their goods to ours, and getting himself much disliked by all the Europeans under him, and hated by the natives, especially by the boat-boys, who were a race or tribe by themselves, coming from one particular part of the coast. He had, of course, been obliged to order the dismissal

of many of them, and this was one reason why they
hated him; but the chief cause was his treatment
of Sooka, the patrao. That man never forgave
Mr. Bransome for beating him so unjustly; and
the news of the deed had travelled very quickly,
as news does in savage countries, so that I think
nearly all Sooka's countrymen knew of the act and
resented it.

Mr. Bransome was quite unaware of the antip-
athy he had thus created toward himself, except so
far as Sooka was concerned; and him he never employed when he had to go off to vessels or land
from them, but always went in the other boat belonging to the factory, which was steered by a
much younger negro. In addition to humbling
Sooka in this way, Bransome took the opportunity of disgracing him whenever he could do so.
Therefore, one day when two pieces of cloth from
the cargo-room were found in the boatmen's huts,
it was no surprise to me that Sooka was at once
fastened upon by Mr. Bransome as the thief who
had stolen them, and that he was tied to the flog-
ging-post in the middle of the yard, and sentenced
to receive fifty lashes with the cat that was kept
for such a purpose, and all without any inquiry
being made. In vain did the unfortunate man
protest his innocence. A swarthy Kroot-boy from
Cape Coast laid the cat on his brown shoulders
right willingly, for he also was an enemy of Sooka's;
and in a few minutes the poor fellow's flesh was cut
and scored as if by a knife.

After the flogging was over Mr. Bransome
amused himself by getting out his rifle and firing
fancy shots at Sooka, still tied to the post; that
is, he tried to put the bullets as close to the poor
wretch as he could without actually wounding him.
To a negro, with his dread of firearms, this was
little short of absolute torture, and at each discharge Sooka writhed and crouched as close to the
ground as he could, while his wide-opened eyes and
mouth, and face of almost a slate colour, showed
how terribly frightened he was. To Mr. Bransome
it appeared to be fine sport, for he fired at least
twenty shots at the man before he shouldered his
rifle and went indoors. Jackson said nothing to
this stupid exhibition of temper, but as soon as it
was over he had Sooka released; and I knew he
attended to his wounds himself, and poured friar's-
balsam into them, and covered his back with a soft
shirt—for all which, no doubt, the negro was afterward grateful. Whether Mr. Bransome got to
know of this, and was offended at it, I do not
know, but shortly afterward he ceased to live
with us.

There was between the factory and the sea, and
a little to the right of the former, a small wooden
cottage which had been allowed to fall into a
dilapidated state from want of some one to live in
it. This Mr. Bransome gave orders to the native
carpenters to repair and make weather-tight; and
when they had done so, he caused a quantity of
furniture to be brought from St. Paul de Loanda

and placed within it. Then he transferred himself and his baggage to the cottage.

Jackson displayed complete indifference to this change on the part of the agent. In fact, there had been, ever since the arrival of the latter upon the Point, and in spite of apparent friendliness, a perceptible breach, widening daily, between the two men. As to the reason of this I had my own suspicions, for I had made the discovery that Jackson had for some time past been drinking very heavily.

In addition to the brandy which we white men had for our own use, I had, to my horror, found out that he was secretly drinking the coarse and fiery rum that was sold to the natives; and as I remembered the mutterings and moanings that had formerly alarmed me, I wondered that I had not guessed the cause of them at the time; but until the arrival of Mr. Bransome, Jackson had always kept charge of the spirits himself, and he was such a secret old fellow that there was no knowing what he had then taken. Now that I was aware of his failing, I was very sorry for the old sailor; for on such a coast and in such a climate there was only one end to it; and although I could not actually prevent him from taking the liquor, I resolved to watch him, and if such symptoms as I had seen before again appeared, to tell Mr. Bransome of them at all hazards. But I was too late to prevent what speedily followed my discovery. It had come about that the same mail-steamer that had brought out Mr. Bransome had again anchored off the

Point, and again the weather was coarse and low-ering. A stiff breeze had blown for some days, which made the rollers worse than they had been for a long while. Both Mr. Bransome and Jackson watched the weather with eager looks, but each was differently affected by it. Bransome appeared to be anxious and nervous, while Jackson was ex-cited, and paced up and down the veranda, and kept, strange to say, for it was contrary to his late habit, a watch upon Bransome's every movement.

Every now and then, too, he would rub his hands together as if in eager expectation, and would chuckle to himself as he glanced seaward. Of his own accord he gave orders to Sooka to get both the surf-boats ready for launching, and to make the boys put on their newest loin-cloths; and then, when everything was in readiness, he asked Bransome if he was going off to the steamer.

"I fear I must," said Bransome; "but I—I don't like the look of those cursed rollers."

At this Jackson laughed, and said something about "being afraid of very little."

"The beach is perfectly good," he added; "Sooka knows, and Sooka is the oldest patrao on the Point."

And Sooka, who was standing by, made a low obeisance to the agent, and said that "the beach lived for well," which was his way of expressing in English that the sea was not heavy.

At that moment a gun was fired from the steamer as a signal to be quick, and Bransome said, "I will go, but not in that black blackguard's boat; it need not come," and he went down to the beach.

It was one of Jackson's rules that when a boat went through the surf there should be some one to watch it, so I walked to the end of the Point to see the agent put off. He got away safely; and I, seeing Sooka's boat lying on the beach, and thinking that it would be as well to have it hauled up under the boat-shed, was on the point of returning to the factory to give the necessary order, when, to my surprise, I saw the boat's crew rush down the beach to the boat and begin to push it toward the sea.

I waved my arms as a signal to them to stop, but they paid no attention to me; and I saw them run the boat into the water, jump into her, and pull off, all singing a song to their stroke in their own language, the sound of which came faintly up to the top of the Point. "Stupid fellows!" I muttered to myself, "they might have known that the boat was not wanted;" and I was again about to turn away, when I was suddenly seized from behind, and carried to the very edge of the cliff, and then as suddenly released.

I sprang to one side, and turning round saw Jackson, with a look of such savage fury on his face that I retreated a step or two in astonishment at him. He perceived my alarm, and burst out into a fit of laughter, which, instead of reassuring me, had the opposite effect, it was so demoniacal in character. "Ha! ha!" he laughed

again, "are you frightened?" and advancing toward me, he put his face close to mine, peering
into it with bloodshot eyes, while his breath, reeking of spirits, poured into my nostrils.

Involuntarily I put up my arm to keep him off.
He clutched it, and, pointing with his other hand
to the sea, whispered hoarsely, "What do you hear
of the surf? Will the breakers be heavier before
sundown? See how they begin to curve! Listen
how they already thunder, thunder, on the beach!
I tell you they are impatient—they seek some
one," he shouted. "Do you know," he continued,
lowering his voice again, and speaking almost con-
fidentially, "sooner or later some one is drowned
upon that bar?" And even as he spoke a fresh line
of breakers arose from the deep, farther out than
any had been before. This much I observed, but
I was too greatly unnerved by the strange manner
of Jackson to pay further heed to the sea. It had
flashed across my mind that he was on the verge
of an attack of delirium tremens, from the effects
of the liquor he had been consuming for so long,
and the problem was to get him back to the house
quietly.

Suddenly a thought struck me. Putting my
arm within his, I said, as coolly as I could, "Never
mind the sea, Jackson; let us have a *matabicho*"
(our local expression for a "drink"). He took the
bait, and came away quietly enough to the house.
Once there, I enticed him into the dining-room,
and shutting to the door quickly, I locked it on

the outside, resolving to keep him there until Mr. Bransome should return; for, being alone, I was afraid of him.

Then I went back to the end of the Point to look for the return of the two boats. When I reached it I saw that the rollers had increased in size in the short time that I had been absent, and that they were breaking, one after another, as fast as they could come shoreward; not pygmy waves, but great walls of water that seemed from their height actually to waver along their huge length before they fell.

A surf such as I had never yet seen had arisen. I stood and anxiously watched through a glass the boats at the steamer's side, and at length, to my relief, I saw one of them leave her, but as it came near I saw, to my surprise, that Mr. Bransome was not in the boat, and that it was not the one that Sooka steered. Quickly it was overtaken by the breakers, but escaped their power, and came in-shore on the back of a majestic roller that did not break until it was close to the beach, where the boat was in safety.

Not without vague apprehension at his impru-dence, but still not anticipating any actual harm from it, I thought that Mr. Bransome had chosen to come back in Sooka's boat, and I waited and waited to see *it* return, although the daylight had now so waned that I could no longer distinguish what was going on alongside the steamer. At last I caught sight of the boat, a white speck upon the

waters, and, just as it entered upon the dangerous
part of the bar, I discerned, to my infinite amaze-
ment, that two figures were seated in the stern—a
man and a woman—a white woman; I could see
her dress fluttering in the wind, and Sooka's black
figure standing behind her.

On came the boat, impelled by the swift-flowing
seas, and for a quarter of an hour it was tossed on
the crests of the waves. Again and again it rose
and sank with them as they came rolling in, but
somehow, after a little further time, it seemed to
me that it did not make such way toward the
shore as it should have done.

I lifted the glass to my eyes, and I saw that the
boys were hardly pulling at all, though the boat
was now close to the rocks that were near the cliff.
Nor did Sooka seem to be conscious of a huge
roller that was swiftly approaching him. In my
excitement I was just on the point of shouting to
warn those in the boat of their danger, although I
knew that they could not understand what I might
say, when I saw Jackson standing on the edge of
the cliff, a little way off, dressed in his shirt and
trousers only. He had escaped from the house!
He perceived that I saw him, and came running
up to me, and I threw myself on my guard. However, he did not attempt to touch me, but stopped
and cried:

" Did I not tell you that somebody would be
drowned by those waves? Watch that boat! watch
it! it is doomed; and the scoundrel, the villain, who

is in it will never reach the shore alive!" and he
hissed the last word through his clinched teeth.

" Good God, Jackson!" I said, " don't say that!
Look, there is a white woman in the boat!"

At the words his jaw dropped, his form, which
a moment before had swayed with excitement, became rigid, and his eyes stared at me as if he
knew, but comprehended not, what I had said.
Then he slowly turned his face toward the sea,
and, as he did so, the mighty breaker that had
been coming up astern of the boat curled over it.
For a moment or two it rushed forward, a solid
body of water, carrying the boat with it; and in
those moments I saw, to my horror, Sooka give one
sweep with his oar, which threw the boat's side toward the roller.   I saw the boat-boys leap clear
of the boat into the surf; I saw the agonised faces
of the man and the woman upturned to the wave
above them, and then the billow broke, and nothing was seen but a sheet of frothy water.   The boat
and those in it had disappeared.   For the crew
I had little concern—I knew they would come
ashore safely enough; but for Mr. Bransome and
the woman, whoever she was, there was little hope.
They had not had time to throw themselves into
the sea before the boat had capsized, and their
clothing would sink them in such a surf, even if
they had escaped being crushed by the boat.   Besides, I feared there had been some foul play on
the part of Sooka.   Quickly as he had done it, I
had seen him with his oar put the boat beyond the

possibility of escaping from the wave, and I remembered how he had been treated by Bransome.

With such thoughts I ran along the cliff to the
pathway that led down to the beach; and as I ran,
I saw Jackson running before me, not steadily or
rightly, but heavily, and swaying from side to side
as he went. Quickly I passed him, but he gave
no sign that he knew any one was near him; and
as I leaped down on to the first ledge of rock
below me, I saw that he was not following me,
but had disappeared among the brushwood.

When I got down to the beach, I found that the
boat's crew had reached the shore in safety, but of
the two passengers nothing had been seen. The
capsized boat was sometimes visible as it lifted on
the rollers, but through my glass I saw that no one
was clinging to it. I called for Sooka, but Sooka
was missing. Every one had seen him land, but
he had disappeared mysteriously. In vain I questioned the other boys as to the cause of the dis-
aster. The only answer I could get out of them
was an appeal to look at the sea and judge for myself. The woman was a white woman from the big
ship, was all they could say about her; and, negro-
like, they evidently considered the loss of a woman
or so of very little consequence.

All I could do was to set a watch along the
beach to look for the bodies when they should be
washed ashore, and this done, I returned to the
factory. My next desire was to find Sooka. He
could hardly have gone far, so I sent for a runner

to take a message to the native king under whose
protection we on the Point were, and after whom
the Point was called, and who was bound to find
the missing man for me if he could, or if he had
not been bribed to let him pass.

In my sorrow at what had happened, and in my
doubt as to the cause of it, I had forgotten all
about Jackson; but after I had despatched my
messenger to the king, I went to look for him. I
discovered him crouching in a corner of his own
bedroom in the dark.

"Are they found?" he asked, in a voice so
hollow and broken that I hardly knew it; and before I could answer him, he whispered to himself,
"No, no; they are drowned—drowned."

I tried to lead him into the lighted dining-room,
but he only crouched the closer to his corner. At
length by the promise of the ever-potent tempta-
tion, liquor, I got him to leave the room. He
could scarcely walk, though, now, and he trembled
so violently that I was glad to give him part of a
bottle of brandy that I had by me. He filled a
tumbler half full of the spirits, and drank it off.
This put strength into him, and for a little he was
calm; but as he again and again applied himself
to the bottle, he became drunk, and swore at me
for my impudence in giving orders without his
sanction. On this I tried to take the bottle from
him, but he clutched it so firmly that I had to let
it go; whereupon he immediately put it to his lips
and swallowed the rest of the liquor that was in it.

After which he gave a chuckle, and staggered to a couch, on which he tumbled, and lay with his eyes open for a long while. At last he fell asleep, but I was too nervous to do likewise, and sat watching him the most of the night; at least, when I awoke it was daylight, and it seemed to me that I had been asleep but a few minutes.

Jackson was still lying on the couch, and his face was calm and peaceful as he softly breathed. The morning, too, was fine, and as I walked on to the veranda I saw the sea sparkling in the sunlight, and there was not a sound from it save a far-off and drowsy murmur. Not a sign remained on its broad surface of the wrath of the day before. It was wonderfully calm. Lying here and there on the veranda, rolled up in their clothes, were the servants of the factory, sleeping soundly on the hard planks.

Presently, as the sun rose in the heavens and warmed the air, the place began to show signs of life, and one of the watch that I had set on the beach came running across the yard to tell me that the bodies had come ashore.

Immediately upon hearing this I called the hammock-bearers together, and going down to the beach, I went a considerable way along it toward a dark spot, which I knew to be a group of natives. On coming up to the group, I found at least fifty negroes collected round the drowned man and woman, all chattering and squabbling among themselves, and probably over the plunder, for I

saw that the bodies had been stripped to their
underclothing.   Rushing into the crowd, with the
aid of a stick I dispersed it, so far as to make the
wretches stand back.   The man, of course, was
Bransome, there was no doubt as to that, although
he had received a terrible blow on the left temple,
most likely from the pointed stem of the boat as it
had toppled over upon him, and his face was dis-
torted and twisted to one side.   The woman was
evidently English, young and pretty, although her
long hair, heavy and wet, was polluted by the sand
that stuck to it, and her half-open eyes were filled
with the same.   On her lips there lingered a slight
smile.   She was of middle height, of slender figure,
and delicately nurtured, as the small bare feet and
little hands showed.   As I looked at the latter I
saw a wedding-ring on her finger, and I thought,
"It is Bransome's wife."   I tried to take the ring
away, but it would not come off her finger—which
I might have known, because the natives would
not have left it there had they been able to remove
it.   I then ordered the bearers to lay the bodies
in the hammocks; and that done, our little party
wended its way along the shore homeward, while
the natives I had dispersed followed one after another in African fashion.

Arrived at the factory, I bade the boys place
the bodies side by side on a spare bed in an empty
room, and then I sent them to dig a grave in the
little burial-ground on the Point, where two or
three worm-eaten wooden crosses marked the

resting-places of former agents of Messrs. Flint Brothers.

As quick interment was necessary in such a climate, even on that very day, I went to call Jackson in order that he might perform the duty that was his—that of reading the burial service over the dead, and of sealing up the desk and effects of Mr. Bransome. But Jackson was not in the factory. I guessed, however, where he was; and sure enough I found him in his accustomed haunt at the end of the Point. The moment he saw me he tried to hide himself among the brush-wood, but I was too quick for him, and spied him as he crouched behind a dwarf palm.

"I know, I know," he cried, as I ran up to him; "I saw you come along the beach. Bury them, bury them out of sight."

"Come, Mr. Jackson," I replied, "it is n't fair to put all the trouble on to me. I am sure I have had enough of the weariness and anxiety of this sad business. You must take your share of it. I want you to read the service for the dead over them."

"No, no," he almost shrieked; "bury them quick; never mind me. Put them out of sight."

"I will not," I said, resolutely. "For your own sake you must, at any rate, view the bodies."

"They have not been murdered?" he replied. But the startled look with which I received the suggestion his words implied seemed to make him recollect himself, for he rose and took my arm with-

out saying more. As he did so, I felt for the first
time a sort of repugnance toward him. Up to
that moment my feeling had been one of pity and
anxiety on his account, but now I loathed him.
This he seemed instinctively to feel, and he clung
closely to me.

Once at the factory I determined that there
should be no more delay on his part, and I took
him to the door of the room where the bodies had
been laid, but at it he made a sudden halt and
would not enter. Covering his face with his
hands, he trembled violently as I pushed the door
open and advanced to the bedside. The room,
hushed and in semi-darkness; the white sheet,
whose surface showed too plainly the forms beneath it; and the scared, terrified face of the man
who, with brain afire, stood watching, with staring eyes, the bed, made a scene I have never forgotten.

Slowly I turned down the upper part of the
sheet, and Jackson, as if fascinated by the act,
advanced a step or two into the room, but with
face averted. Gradually he turned it toward the
bodies, and for a moment his gaze rested upon
them. The next instant he staggered forward,
looked at the woman's face, panted for breath once
or twice, and then, with uplifted hands and a wild
cry of "Lucy!" fell his length upon the floor.
When I stooped over him he was in convulsions,
and dark matter was oozing out of his mouth.
The climax had come. I shouted for the servants,

and they carried him to his own room, and placed him on his own bed.

How I got through that day I hardly know. Alone I buried Bransome and his wife, and alone I returned from the hurried task to watch by Jackson's bedside. None of the natives would stay near him. For two days he lay unconscious. At the end of that time he seemed to have some idea of the outside world, for his eyes met mine with intelligence in their look, and on bending over him I heard him whisper, " Forgive me! " Then he relapsed into unconsciousness again. Through the long hours his eyes remained ever open and restless; he could not eat, nor did he sleep, and I was afraid he would pass away through weakness without a sign, being an old man. On the third day he became delirious, and commenced chattering and talking to himself, and imagining that all kinds of horrid shapes and creatures were around and near him. I had to watch him narrowly in order to prevent him stealing out of his bed, which he was ready to do at any moment to avoid the tortures which he fearfully imagined awaited him. By these signs I knew that he was in the middle of an attack of delirium tremens, and I tried to quiet him by means of laudanum, but it had no effect upon him. I got him, however, to swallow a little soup, which sustained him. My own boy was the only negro I had been able to induce to stay in the room, and he would only remain in it while I was there.

I had sent a messenger to the nearest station,
where I remembered there was a Portuguese doctor; but he had not returned by the evening of the
fourth day. That night, worn out with watching,
I had dozed off to sleep on a chair placed by the
sick man's bed, when all at once I was awakened
by a loud report, and I jumped up to find the
room filled with smoke. As it cleared away I
saw that Jackson was standing in the middle of
the room with a revolver in his hand. As I con-
fronted him he laughed a devilish laugh and cocked
the weapon, crying as he did so, "It was you
who tempted me with your smooth face and un-
suspicious way, and you shall die, though I suffer
doubly in hell for it. Hist!" and he stopped suddenly and listened. "Don't you hear the breakers? Hark, how they roar! They say they are
ready, always ready," and staring in front of him,
he advanced, as if following the sign of an invisible hand, to the door, unconsciously placing, to my
infinite relief, the revolver on the top of a chest of
drawers as he passed by it. I did not dare to
move, and he opened the door and walked into
the front room. Then I followed him. For a little
he remained in the room, glaring vacantly about
him, and muttering to himself; but seeing the
outer door open he made a rush toward it, and
disappeared into the darkness of the night. Calling to the boy, I ran after him, and easily came up
to him, when he turned, and picking up a heavier
stone than I thought he could have lifted, threw it

at me. I dodged it and closed with him. Once
in my arms I found I could hold him, and my servant and I carried him back into the factory. We
placed him on the floor of the dining-room, and
he was too exhausted to move for a while. By
degrees, however, he recovered sufficiently to
stand; and as soon as he could do so by himself,
with devilish cunning he made for the lamp, which
he struck, quick as lightning, with a stick that had
been lying on the table. In an instant the great
round globe fell to pieces, but luckily the chimney
was not broken, and the lamp remained alight, and
before he could strike another blow at it I had
grappled with him again. This time he struggled
violently for a few moments, and seemed to think
that he was dealing with Bransome, for he shrieked,
" What! have you come back from the sea? You
are wet! you are wet!" and shuddering, he tried
to free himself from my hold; and I, not liking to
hurt him, let him go, taking care to keep myself
between him and the lamp.

" Back from me, you villain of hell!" he cried,
as soon as he was free. " What have you done
with her? what have you done with her? " And
then, in a tone of weird and pathetic sorrow,
" Where is my little one that I loved? I have
sought her many a year; oh, why did she forsake
me? Aha, Sooka! we were right to send him to
the hell whence he came—the lying, false-hearted
scoundrel, to steal away my white dove!"

After which he drew from his finger a solid gold

ring which he always wore, and threw it from him, saying, with a wild laugh, " There! that 's for any one that likes it; I 'm a dead man." He then staggered toward his own room, and I, remembering the loaded revolver which still lay on the chest of drawers, tried to intercept him. In his rage, for I verily believe that he also remembered that the weapon was there, he spat in my face, and struck me with all his force between the eyes; but I stuck to him, and with the help of the boy, who had been all this time in hiding, but who came forward at my call, I laid him for the last time upon his bed. There he lay exhausted for the remainder of the night; but there was no rest for me; I felt that I had to watch him now for my own safety.

Toward morning, however, his breathing became, all at once, very heavy and slow, and I bent over him in alarm. As I did so, I heard him sigh faintly, " Lucy!" and at that moment the native boy softly placed something upon the bed. I took it up. It was the ring the sick man had thrown away in the night, and as I looked at it I saw " James, from Lucy " engraved on its inside surface, and I knew that the dead woman was his wife.

As the first faint streaks of dawn stole into the room, the slow-drawn breathing of the dying man ceased. I listened—it came again—once—twice —and then all was silence. He was dead, and I realised in the sudden stillness that had come upon the room that I was alone. Yet he had passed away so quietly after his fitful fever that I could not bring myself to believe that he was really gone, and I stood looking at the body, fearing to convince myself of the truth by touching it.

So entranced was I by that feeling of awe which comes to almost every one in the presence of death, that I did not hear the shouting of the hammock-boy outside, or the footsteps of a white man coming into the room; and not until he touched me on the shoulder did I turn and recognise the sallow face of the Portuguese doctor whom I had sent for, and who had thus arrived too late. However, he served to help me to bury the mortal part of Jackson in the little graveyard beside the body of his wife and that of the man who had come between them when alive. And such was without doubt the fact; for when the doctor had gone, and I was alone again, I collected and made an inventory of the dead men's effects, and in Jackson's desk I found his diary, or, as he himself would have called it, his log; and in that log was noted, on the very day that Bransome had arrived on the Point, his suspicion of the man, and later on his conviction that Bransome was indeed he who had injured him.

Sooka was never found; but when the mail-steamer returned from the south coast, I discovered that the younger patrao had made his crew row away suddenly from the steamer's side, while Mr. Bransome had been engaged below, and was out of sight. So it was evident that the pair had been in league together to insure Sooka his revenge. What share Jackson had had in the murder of his enemy I did not care to think of, but feared the worst.

For myself, I had to remain on the Point for many months, until the factory was finally closed —for no purchaser was ever found for it; and doubtless, by this time, the buildings are in ruins, and long grass hides the graves of those who sleep upon King Bemba's Point.

GHAMBA

BY

WILLIAM CHARLES SCULLY

GHAMBA

BY WILLIAM CHARLES SCULLY

The darksome cave they enter, where they find
That cursèd man, low sitting on the ground,
Musing full sadly in his sullen mind.
The Faërie Queene.

WHEN Corporal Francis Dollond and Trooper
James Franks, of the Natal Mounted Police,
overstayed their ten days' leave of absence from
the camp on the Upper Tugela, in the early part
of 1883, everybody was much surprised; they being two of the best conducted and most methodi-
cal men in the force. But the weeks and then the
months went by without anything whatever being
heard of them, so they were officially recorded as
deserters. Nevertheless none of their comrades
really believed that these men had deserted; each
one felt there was something mysterious about the
circumstance of their disappearance. They had
applied for leave for the alleged purpose of visiting Pietermaritzburg. They started on foot, stat-
ing their intention of walking to Estcourt, hiring
horses from natives there, and proceeding on

horseback. They had evidently never reached
Estcourt, as nothing could be heard of them at
that village. They were both young men—colo-
nists by birth. Dollond had an especially youthful
appearance. Franks was older. He had joined
the force later in life. He and Dollond, who had
only very recently before his disappearance been
promoted, were chums.

Some months later in the same year, when
Troopers George Langley and Hiram Whitson
also applied for ten days' leave of absence,—likewise to proceed to Pietermaritzburg,—the leave
was granted; but the officer in charge of the detachment laughingly remarked that he hoped they
were not going to follow Dollond and Franks.

Now, neither Langley nor Whitson had the re-
motest idea of visiting Pietermaritzburg. It is
necessary, of course, for the reader to know where
they did intend going to, and how the intention
arose; but before doing this we must deal with
some antecedent circumstances.

Langley was most certainly the most boyish-
looking man in the force. He had a perfectly
smooth face, ruddy complexion, and fair hair. He
was of middle height, and was rather inclined to
stoutness. He was so fond of talking that his
comrades nicknamed him " Magpie." A colonist
by birth, he could speak the Kaffir language like a
native.

Whitson was a sallow-faced, spare-built man of
short stature, with dark-brown beard and hair, and

piercing black eyes. His age was about forty.
He had a wiry and terrier-like appearance. A
"down-East" Yankee, he had spent some years in
Mexico, and then drifted to South Africa during
the war period, which, it will be remembered, lasted
from 1877 to 1882. He had served in the Zulu
war as a non-commissioned officer in one of the
irregular cavalry corps, with some credit. The
fact of his being a man of extremely few words
was enough to account for the friendship which
existed between him and the garrulous Langley.
Whitson was known to be a dead shot with the
revolver.

This is how they came to apply for leave: One
day Langley was strolling about just outside the
lines, looking for somebody to talk to, when he
noticed an apparently very old native man sitting
on an ant-heap and regarding him somewhat intently. This old native had been several times seen
in the vicinity of the camp, but he never seemed to
speak to any one, and he looked so harmless that
the police did not even trouble to ask him for the
written pass which all natives are obliged by law
to carry when they move about the country. The
old man saluted Langley and asked in his own
language for a pipeful of tobacco. Langley always carried some loose leaves broken up in his
pocket, so he at once pulled some of these out and
half filled the claw-like hand outstretched to receive them. The old native was voluble in his
thanks. There was a large ant-heap close to the

one on which he had been sitting, and on which
he reseated himself while filling his pipe. Against
this Langley leaned and took a good look at his
companion. The man had a most extraordinary
face. His lower jaw and cheek-bones were largely
developed, but Langley hardly noticed this, so
struck was he with the strange formation of the
upper jaw. That portion of the superior maxillary
bone which lies between the sockets of the eye-
teeth protruded, with the sockets, to a remarkable
degree, and instead of being curved appeared to
be quite straight. The incisor teeth were very
large and white, but it was the development of the
eye-teeth that was most startling. These, besides
being very massive, were produced below the level
of the incisors to a depth of nearly a quarter of an
inch. They distinctly suggested to Langley the
tusks of a baboon.

As is not very unusual with natives, the man
was perfectly bald. His back was bent, and his
limbs were somewhat shrunken, but he did not appear in the least degree decrepit. His eyelids were
very red, and his eyes, though dim, had a deep and
intent look. Ugly as was the man—or perhaps by
virtue of his ugliness—he exercised a strange fas-
cination over Langley.

The old man, whose name turned out to be
Ghamba, proved himself a talker after Langley's
own heart. They discussed all sorts of things.
Ghamba startled his hearer by his breadth of experience and his shrewdness. He said he was a

"Hlubi" Kaffir from Qumbu, in the territory of
Griqualand East, but that he had for some time
past been living in Basutoland, which is situated
just behind the frowning wall of the Drakensberg,
to the southwest of where they were speaking, and
not twenty miles distant.

They talked until it was time for Langley to return to camp. He was so pleased at the entertainment afforded by Ghamba that all the tobacco he
had with him found its way into the claw-like hand
of that strange-looking man of many experiences
and quaint ideas. So Langley asked him to come
to the ant-heap again on the following day, and
have another talk at the same hour. This Ghamba,
with a wide and prolonged exposure of his teeth,
readily agreed to do.

Langley was extremely voluble to Whitson that
night over his new acquaintance. Whitson listened
with his usual impassiveness, and then asked Langley how it was that "an old loafing nigger," as he
expressed it, had impressed him so remarkably.
Langley replied that he did not quite know, but
he thought the effect was largely due to the man's
teeth. But all the same he was "a very entertain-
ing old buffer."

Next afternoon Langley was so impatient to re-
sume conversation with his new friend that he re-
paired to the ant-heap quite half an hour before
the appointed time. He had not, however, long
to wait, as Ghamba soon appeared, emerging from
a donga a couple of hundred yards away.

Langley was more impressed than ever. Ghamba told him all about the Basutos, among whom he had lived; about the old days in Natal, before even the Dutch occupation, when Tshaka's impis wiped whole tribes out of existence; of the recent wars in Zululand and the Cape Colony, and as to the probability of future disturbances. Charmed as was Langley by the old man's conversation, he felt that on this occasion there was a little too much of it; that Ghamba was not nearly so good a listener as he had been on the previous day; so when the latter at length put a question to him, thus affording an opportunity for the exercise of his own pent-up loquacity, Langley felt elated, more especially as several inquiries were grouped together in the one asking. Ghamba asked whether anything had been heard of Umhlonhlo; whether the capture of that fugitive rebel was considered likely, and whether it was true that a reward of five hundred pounds had been offered by the government for his capture, dead or alive.

Umhlonhlo, it will be remembered, was the Pondomise chief who rebelled in 1880, treacherously murdered Mr. Hope, the magistrate of Qumbu, and his two companions, and who has since been an outlaw with a price on his head.

Langley replied to the effect that it was quite true such a reward had been offered; that nothing as yet had been ascertained as to Umhlonhlo's whereabouts, but that the government believed him to be in Pondoland; that he was sure to be

captured eventually; that he, Langley, only wished
he knew where Umhlonhlo was, so as to have the
chance of making five hundred pounds with which
to buy a certain nice little farm he knew of; and
that should he ever succeed in obtaining the reward, and consequently in taking his discharge
and purchasing the farm, he would be jolly glad
if old Ghamba would come and live with him.
This is only some of what he said; when Langley's
tongue got into motion, he seemed to have some
difficulty in stopping it.

However, he paused at last, and then Ghamba,
looking very intently at him, said:

"Look here, can you keep a secret?"

Here was a mystery.

"Rather!" said Langley.

"Will you swear by the name of God that you
will not reveal what I have to tell you?"

Langley swore.

Ghamba drew near until his teeth were within
a few inches of Langley's cheek, and said in a
whisper:

"I know where Umhlonhlo is."

Langley started, and said in an awed voice:

"Where is he?"

"Wait a bit," said Ghamba; "perhaps I will
tell you, and perhaps I won't. I like you; you
have given me tobacco, and you are not too proud
to come and talk to a poor old man. Now, you
say you would like to make five hundred pounds
and buy a farm?"

"Rather!"

"And that you would let me go and live on the farm with you and end my days in peace?"

"I would, gladly."

"Well then, if I take you to where Umhlonhlo is, and you kill him and get the money, will you give me twenty-five pounds, and let me keep a few goats, and grow a few mealies on your land?"

"I should think I would. But how could one man take or kill Umhlonhlo? They say he is well armed and that he has a lot of followers with him."

"Umhlonhlo," said Ghamba, glancing anxiously round as if he feared the very ant-heaps were listening, "is hiding in a cave in the mountains, not three days' walk from here. He has not got a single man with him, because he fears being given up. He is really in hiding from his own followers now. My sister is one of his wives, and that is how I know all about it. I passed the cave where he lives four nights ago, and saw him sitting by the fire. He has only a few women with him."

"And how do you think I should take him?"

"Take him? you should kill him. I will guide you to the cave by night, and then you can shoot him as he sits by the fire."

Langley, although no coward, was not particularly brave. He did not much relish the idea of alone tackling the redoubtable Umhlonhlo, a savage of muscle, who was reported to be always armed to the teeth. Moreover, he had no gun,

and was but an indifferent shot with a revolver.
So he thought over the matter for a few moments
and then said :

"Look here, Ghamba ; I do not care to tackle
this job alone, but if I can take another man with
me, I am on."

"Then you will only get half of the five hundred
pounds, and will not be able to buy the farm. You
need not be afraid ; you can shoot him without his
seeing you."

"No," said Langley, after a pause ; "I will not
go alone, but if you will let me take another man
with me, it can be managed. It will make no
difference to you ; you will get your twenty-five
pounds."

"And how about my going to live on the farm
with you? "

"Well, I could not buy the farm for two hundred and fifty pounds. Come, we will give you
fifty pounds instead of twenty-five."

Ghamba thought for a while and then said :

"Very well, I consent. But there need be only
one other man, and you will write down on a
piece of paper that you will give me the fifty
pounds. When can we start ? "

"I must speak to the other man, and then we
will apply for leave. We had better start soon, or
else Umhlonhlo may have gone to some other place
of hiding."

"Yes, we must lose no time."

"All right! Meet me here to-morrow and I

will bring my friend. We will then settle all about it."

"You must not mention this matter to any one else, and you must make your friend promise to keep the secret."

"Oh, that 's all right!" said Langley. "Meet me here to-morrow, just after dinner."

Langley went back to camp, Ghamba looking after his retreating figure with a smile that revealed his teeth in a very striking manner. Langley was intensely excited, and exacted (quite unnecessarily) the most solemn promises from Whitson not to divulge the great secret which he confided to him. Whitson agreed at once to join in the enterprise, which was one after his own heart.

Next day the three met at the big ant-heap, and Whitson was very much impressed by Ghamba's teeth. He told Langley afterward that they reminded him of a picture of the devil which he had seen in a copy of the "Pilgrim's Progress." The old man's story appeared, however, consistent enough, in spite of his peculiar dentition.

So, after a short conversation, Langley and Whitson returned to camp, having made an appointment to meet Ghamba again on the following morning at sunrise, so as to finally arrange as to time of starting, etc. They went at once to the officer in charge of the detachment and applied for ten days' leave of absence for the purpose of proceeding to Pietermaritzburg, which was at once granted.

Next morning they met Ghamba again, and agreed to start on their expedition that evening. He explained that they must do all their travelling by night, and lie by during the day; because it would never do for him, Ghamba, to run the risk of being recognised by persons whom they might meet. For the sake of his Hlubi relations who were living among the Pondomise at Qumbu, it was absolutely necessary that he should not appear in the transaction at all. Were it ever to be even suspected that he had betrayed the chief, not alone would he be certainly killed, but all his relations would be shunned by the other natives. He was an old man, so for him, personally, nothing mattered very much, but a man is bound to consider the interests of his family. Travelling only by night, and lying still and hidden during the day, were therefore absolutely necessary stipulations, and Langley and Whitson agreed to them as intelligible and reasonable. All being settled, the latter started for the camp, Ghamba baring his teeth excessively as they walked away.

At dusk on the evening of the same day, Langley and Whitson met Ghamba once more at the large ant-heap, and the three at once proceeded on their course. The only arms taken were revolvers of the government regulation pattern (breech-loading central fire). They carried provisions calculated to last eight days, but took no blankets on account of having to travel at night. When

Ghamba volunteered to relieve them of a considerable share of their respective loads, Langley and Whitson were filled with grateful surprise.

The plan was as follows: Whitson was to shoot Umhlonhlo, and then remain in the cave while Langley returned to the camp to report what had been done, and cause persons who could identify the body to be sent for. They seem to have had no scruples as to the deed they meant to do; certainly Umhlonhlo deserved no more mercy than a beast of prey. Nor does it seem to have struck them that possibly they might shoot the wrong man. But there was an air of conviction about the manner in which Ghamba showed his teeth when asked whether he was positive as to the identity of the man in the cave, that would have dissipated the doubts of most men. Besides this, he drew out the written undertaking which they had delivered to him, and said, with a profoundly businesslike look:

"Do I not want the money? Should I take all this trouble if I did not know what I were doing?"

They walked all night, only resting once or twice for a few minutes. It was found that Ghamba, in spite of his age, was an extremely good walker; and when they halted at daylight, Langley was so done up that he could not have held out for another half-hour. Whitson, the wiry, had not yet felt the least fatigue.

This march had taken them to the very foot of the Drakensberg range, and they rested in a valley between two of its main spurs. Here they remained all day, comfortably located in a sheltered nook where there was plenty of dry grass. Their resting-place was encircled by immense rocks. Although the surrounding country was desolate to a degree, and neither a human being nor an animal was to be seen, Ghamba would not hear of their lighting a fire nor leaving the spot where they rested. The weather was clear, and neither too warm nor too cold. They slept at intervals during the day, and at evening felt quite recovered from their fatigue.

At nightfall they again started, their course leading steeply up the gorge in which they had rested. Although the pathway became more and more indistinct, Ghamba appeared never to be at a loss. Langley several times shuddered, when they passed by the very edge of some immense precipice, or clambered along some steep mountain-side, where a false step would have meant destruction. He began to show signs of fatigue soon after midnight, so at Ghamba's suggestion a considerable portion of his load was transferred to the shoulders of Whitson, who seemed to be as tireless as Ghamba himself.

At daybreak they halted in the depths of another tremendous gorge with precipitous sides. The scenery in this particular area of the Drakensberg range, the neighbourhood of the Mont aux Sources, is indescribably grand and impressive, and is quite unlike anything else in South Africa.

Enormous and fantastically shaped mountains are here huddled together indiscriminately, and between them wind and double deep gloomy gorges, along the bottoms of which mighty boulders are thickly strewn. On dizzy ledge and steep slope dense thickets of wild bamboo grow, and a few stunted trees fill some of the less deep clefts, wherever the sunshine can penetrate. Splendid as is the scenery, its gloom, its stillness, its naked crags and peaks, its dark depths that seem to cleave to the very vitals of the earth, become so oppressive that, after a few days spent among them, the traveller is filled with repulsion and almost horror. Few living things have their home there. You might meet an occasional "klipspringer" (an antelope, in habits and appearance somewhat like the chamois), a wandering troop of baboons, and now and then a herd of eland in the more grassy areas. There are said to be a few Bushmen still haunting the caves, but they are seldom or never seen.

In the afternoon the sun shone into the gorge in which the travellers were resting, and for a few hours the heat was very oppressive. Whitson examined his revolver, removing the cartridges and replacing them by others. He then lay down to sleep, asking Langley to remain awake and keep a lookout. He had a vague feeling of uneasiness which he could not overcome. Langley promised to keep awake, but he was too tired to do so. He sat with his back against a rock, and, after some futile efforts to keep his eyes open, fell fast asleep.

By-and-by Ghamba woke him gently, and, pointing to Whitson, whose revolver lay in the leather case close to his hand, whispered:

"Did he not tell you to keep awake?"

Langley was grateful for this evidence of consideration, but he could not quite make out how Ghamba had been able to understand what Whitson had said. However, when the latter awoke, Langley said nothing to him about having disobeyed instructions.

Ghamba said that about two hours' walk would now bring them to Umhlonhlo's cave, so they started off briskly at dusk. Their course now led for some distance along a mountain ledge covered with wild bamboo, through which the pathway wound. Then they crossed a steep saddle between two enormous peaks, after which they plunged into another deep and winding gorge. This they followed until they reached a part where it was so narrow that the sides seemed almost to touch over their heads. Beyond the cliffs fell apart, and then apparently curved toward each other again, thus forming an immense amphitheatre. At the entrance to this Ghamba stopped, and said in a whisper that they were now close to the cave.

They now held a consultation, in terms of which it was decided that Ghamba should go forward and reconnoitre. So Whitson and Langley sat down close together and waited, conversing in low tones.

Whitson felt very uneasy, but Langley tried to argue him out of his fears. The more Whitson saw

of Ghamba, the more he disliked and distrusted
him and his teeth. The instinct which detects
danger in the absence of any apparent evidence
of its existence is a faculty developed in some men
by an adventurous life. This faculty Whitson possessed in a high degree.

"Did you keep awake all the time I slept this
afternoon?" he asked.

Langley feared Whitson and felt inclined to lie,
but something impelled him, almost against his
will, to speak the truth now.

"No," he replied; "I slept for a few minutes."

Whitson drew his revolver and opened the
breech.

"By God!" he said, "the cartridges are gone!"

Langley took his weapon out of the leather case
and opened it. He found the cartridges were
there right enough.

"Have you any spare cartridges?" asked
Whitson.

Whitson had already loaded his revolver with the
five cartridges which he had removed in the afternoon, but he again took these out and replaced
them in his waistcoat pocket, and then he reloaded
with some which Langley passed over to him with
a trembling hand.

"Look here," he said, in a hoarse whisper, "we
are in a trap of some kind. When that old
scoundrel comes back, do not let him know that
we have found out anything. We will walk on with
him for a short distance, at all events, and then be

guided by circumstances. Stand by when you see me collar him, and slip a sack over his head."

" Can we not go back now?" said Langley.

" Certainly not; we would never find our way at night. I guess we must see this circus out. If you have to shoot, aim low."

In a few minutes Ghamba returned.

" Come on," he said. " He is sitting at the fire in front of the cave. I have just seen him."

" Where is the cave?" asked Whitson. " Is it far from here?"

" We will reach it very soon; you can see the light of the fire from a few paces ahead."

They walked on for about fifty yards, and there, sure enough, over a rocky slope to their left, and at the foot of a crag about three hundred yards away, could be seen the bright and fitful glow from a fire which was hidden from their view by a low ridge of piled-up rocks.

Whitson stood still and questioned Ghamba:

" Now tell me," he asked, through Langley as interpreter, " how we are to approach."

" The pathway leads up on the left side," replied Ghamba. " We will walk close up to the crag, where there is a narrow passage between it and that big black rock which you see against the light. You two can lead, and I will be close behind. I have just seen him. He is sitting at the fire, eating, and only the women are with him."

The last words were hardly out of the speaker's

mouth before Whitson had seized him by the throat
with a vice-like grasp.

"Seize his hands and hold them," he hissed to
Langley.

Ghamba struggled desperately, but could not release himself. Whitson compressed his throat until
he became unconscious, and then gagged him with
a pocket-handkerchief. Ghamba's hands were then
tied tightly behind his back with another pocket-
handkerchief, and his feet were firmly secured with
a belt. An empty sack (from which they had removed their provisions) was then drawn over his
head and shoulders, and secured round the waist.

"Come on now, quickly," whispered Whitson,
and he and Langley started off in the direction of
the fire, after first taking off their boots.

They did not approach by the course which
Ghamba had indicated, but made their way
quietly up the slope, straight against the face of
the crag. They reached the heap of rocks, and
crept in among them by means of another narrow
passage, close to the inner end of which the fire
was; and this is what they saw through the twigs
of a scrubby bush which effectually concealed
them:

A large cave opened into the side of the mountain, and just before the mouth was an open space
about twenty yards in diameter, surrounded on all
sides, except that of the mountain itself, by a wall
of loosely piled rocks, through which passages led
out in different directions. Just in front of the

cave burned a bright fire, around which crouched four most hideous and filthy-looking old hags, and against which were propped several large earthenware pots of native make, full of water. Standing behind rocks, one at each side of the inner entrance to the passage, which was evidently that communicating with the pathway indicated by Ghamba as the one they were to approach by, were two powerful-looking men, stark naked, and as black as ebony, their skins shining in the light of the fire. Each man held a coiled thong in his hands, after the manner of a sailor about to heave a line. While they were looking, a woman, somewhat younger in appearance than any of those who sat by the fire, came out of the cave carrying a strong club about three feet long. She crouched down close to the man standing on the left-hand side of the passage, who, as well as his companion, stood as still as a marble statue, and in an expectant attitude.

Whitson and Langley, with their revolvers drawn, suddenly stepped out of their concealment, and walked toward the fire. This evidently disconcerted the men with the thongs, who apparently did not expect their intended prey to approach by any course except the passage near which they were standing; but after a slight pause of hesitancy the thongs were whirling in the air, and descending, lasso-fashion, upon the shoulders of the intruders. The noose caught Langley over his arms, which were instantly drawn close against his body as the thong tightened, so he was thus rendered completely powerless; but Whitson sprang, quick as lightning, to one side, and escaped. Three shots from his revolver rang out in as many seconds, and the two men and the woman —who was in the act of lifting her club to brain Langley—lay rolling on the ground, each with a bullet through the head.

The four old hags at the fire began to mow and scream, and got up and hobbled into the cave. Whitson drew his knife and cut the thong with which Langley was vainly struggling, and then the two men, pale as death, looked silently at each other with starting eyes.

Whitson reloaded his revolver, and then made a sort of torch out of dry reeds, a pile of which lay close at hand. He then, leaving Langley to guard the cave, carefully examined all the passages and spaces between the rocks, but he could find no trace of any one. The two men thereupon entered the cave, Whitson holding the torch high over his head. They found that it ran straight in for about fifteen paces, and then curved sharply to the left.

It was about four paces in width, and about eight feet high, the roof being roughly arched. The walls and roof were covered with thick black greasy soot; and an indescribably horrible stench, which increased the farther they advanced, made them almost vomit. They found that where the cave curved to the left it ended in a circular chamber about eight paces in diameter, and at one side of this crouched the four old hags, huddled together, and mowing and chattering horribly.

Across a cleft about two feet wide, in the right-hand wall of the cave, a stick was fixed transversely, and hanging to this were some lumps of half-dried and smoked flesh. Whitson went up close and examined these carefully. He drew back with a shudder, and his face changed from pale to ashen gray.

He and Langley then went outside and stood for a while in the fresh air. They could endure, just then, no more of the fetid atmosphere inside. After a short time they gathered up some dry twigs and reeds, and set several little heaps alight at different spots inside. This had the effect of making the atmosphere more bearable in the course of a few minutes. They then made a larger fire in the middle of the cave, and proceeded to examine it more closely.

They found several old iron picks, such as are used by natives in cultivating their fields, some very filthy skins, a number of earthenware pots, a few knives, and an axe; but nothing more.

The floor of the cave was of clay, and at one spot it appeared to have been recently disturbed. Here Langley began to dig with a pick, which, just below the surface, struck against some hard substance. This, when uncovered, proved to be a bone. He threw it to one side and dug deeper, uncovering more bones—some old, and others comparatively fresh, but emitting a horrible smell.

He stooped and picked one up, but dropped it immediately, as if it burned him. It was the lower jawbone of a human being.

"Great God!" he gasped. "What is the meaning of this?"

"It means," said Whitson, "that we are in a nest of bloody cannibals!"

Langley dropped like a stone, in a dead faint; so Whitson dragged him outside, and, leaving him to recover in the open air, returned to the cave. He then seized the pick and began digging, unearthing some new horror at every stroke. A glittering object caught his eye; he picked this up and found it to be the steel buckle of a woman's belt. He glanced toward the cleft in the rock where the lumps of flesh were hanging, and caught his breath short. Going outside he made another torch, which he lit; and then he returned and carefully examined the loosened surface. Another glittering object caught his eye. This, when examined, proved to be an old silver watch, the appearance of which seemed familiar. He forced open the case, and saw, roughly scratched on the inside, the letter D. He now recognised it; he remembered having once fixed a glass in this very watch for Dollond, about a month before the latter's disappearance. Continuing his search Whitson found the iron heel-plate of a boot, and a small bunch of keys.

Whitson drew his revolver, and picking up the torch went into the terminal chamber. Four shots, fired in quick succession, reverberated immediately afterward through the cavern.

Whitson then went outside to Langley, whom he found sitting down near the fire, looking, if possible, more ghastly than before. The presence of Whitson seemed, however, to act on him as a kind of tonic, and he soon pulled himself together sufficiently to assist in piling a quantity of fuel upon the already sinking fire, which soon blazed brightly, lighting up the mouth of the cavern and the space in front of it. One of the bodies of the men who had been shot was lying on its side, with the face toward the fire. Whitson examined the mouth, pushing back the upper lip with a piece of stick. He found that the shape of the mouth and the development of the teeth were the same as Ghamba's. The other bodies were lying on their faces, so he did not trouble to examine them.

Whitson then told Langley to follow him, and the two walked down the foot-path toward where they had left Ghamba. Him they found lying motionless in the position in which he had been left about an hour previously. They removed the sack and the gag and untied his feet, first taking the precaution to fasten the belt by one end to his bound hands, Whitson holding the other. They then signed to him to proceed toward the cave, and this he silently did, without making any resistance. He looked calmly at the three dead bodies, but said not a word. Langley held him, while Whitson again tied his feet together with the belt,

and then they placed him with his back against
a rock, facing the fire, which was still blazing
brightly. His lips were drawn back in a ghastly,
mirthless grin, and the tusks were revealed from
point to insertion.

Langley questioned Ghamba, but he would not
speak. After several attempts to force him to answer had been vainly made, Whitson said :

"Now tell him that if he speaks and tells the
whole truth he will only be shot, but if he does not
speak he will be burned alive."

This was interpreted, but the threat had no apparent effect. So Whitson seized Ghamba and
dragged him to the fire, where he flung him down
on the very edge of the glowing embers.

"Now," said Whitson, holding him down with
his foot, so that he got severely scorched, "for the
last time, will you speak? "

"Take me away from the fire, and I will speak,"
said Ghamba, in English.

So they lifted him, and set him again with his
back to the rock.

"Now," said Whitson, "go ahead, and no
nonsense!"

"If I tell the whole truth," said Ghamba, still
speaking English, and with a fair accent, "will
you swear not to burn me, but to shoot me, so that
I shall die at once? "

"I will," said Whitson.

"You too must swear," said Ghamba, looking
at Langley.

"Yes, I swear."

"Very well," said Ghamba, "I will tell you everything, but you must both remember what you have sworn to."

"Yes, all right," said Whitson. Ghamba then looked at Langley, who repeated th ; words.

"I will tell you," said Ghamba, "all I can remember, and you can ask questions, which I shall answer truly. You have heard of Umdava, who used to eat men in Natal long ago, after the wars of Tshaka—well, he was my uncle. After Umdava had been killed and his people scattered, my father, with a few followers, came to live among these mountains. But we found that after having eaten human flesh we could enjoy no other food, so we caught people and ate them. These two men lying dead are my sons, and that woman is my daughter. My four wives were here to-night. They are very old women. Have you not seen them?" he asked, looking at Whitson.

"They are in there ; I shot them," said Whitson, pointing to the cave.

"I had other children," continued Ghamba, quite unmoved, "but we ate them when food was scarce."

"Have you always lived, all these years, on human flesh?" asked Whitson.

"No, not always; but whenever we could obtain it we did so. There is other food in these mountains—honey, ants' eggs, roots, and fruit; besides game, which is, however, not very easy to catch. But we have often all had to go away and work when times have been bad. Besides, I have a herd of cattle at a Basuto kraal, and I have been in the habit of taking some of these now and then, and exchanging them for corn, which the women then went to fetch. But we have always tried to get people to eat, because we could enjoy no other kind of food. Sometimes we got them easily; and when we were very fortunate we used to dry part of the meat by hanging it up and lighting a fire underneath, with green wood, so as to make plenty of smoke."

" Have you killed many white people? " asked Whitson.

" Yes, a good number; but not, of course, as many as black. Lately we have always tried to catch whites, because when you have eaten white flesh for some time, the flesh of a native no longer satisfies you."

" Why not? "

" The flavour is not so strong."

" Did you induce the other two policemen to come up by means of the story about Umhlonhlo? "

" Yes, they came up just as you did, and my sons caught them with the thongs. Umhlonhlo has brought us plenty of food."

" Were you able to take the cartridges out of their revolvers as you did out of mine? "

" No, I had no opportunity; but it was not necessary, because my sons were so expert at throwing the thongs that they could always catch people over the arms, and thus render them unable to shoot."

" How did they manage to become so expert? "

" By continued practice. I used to walk up the path over and over again, and let them throw the thong over me. Then the woman was always there with the club, so that, if one of the thongs missed, she was ready to strike. I, also, was usually ready to help, in case of necessity."

" Why did you think it necessary to take the cartridges out of my revolver? "

" Because I feared you from the first, and were it not that he "—baring his teeth and glancing at Langley, who shuddered—" looked so nice, and that we wanted fresh meat so badly, I would not have risked bringing you. But it would have been all right if I had only let your revolver alone."

" You say Umhlonhlo has brought you plenty of food ; did you ever get any one besides ourselves and the other two policemen to come up here by telling them that story? "

" Yes, two others—one a man who was searching for gold on the Free State side of the mountains, and the other a trader whom I met at Maseru. But these each came alone."

" I see the buckle of a woman's belt in there. Whom did that belong to? You surely never got a white woman up here? "

" Yes, we did," said Ghamba, with a horrible half-smile which bared the gums high above the sockets of his tusks. " She was a young girl who had strayed from a waggon passing over the mountain by the Ladysmith road, only a day's walk from here. I pretended to show her the shortest way to her waggon, and thus brought her as far as she could walk in this direction. I then killed her, and came up here and fetched my sons. We carried her up in the night. She was very young and plump, and I have never eaten anything that I enjoyed so much." (Whitson turned cold with horror. He remembered the girl's mysterious disappearance, and the fruitless searches undertaken in consequence.) "His flesh"—glancing again at Langley—"looks something like hers did, and I am sure it would taste just as nice. There was still a little of her left when I went away last week. If you will go in there and look where the rock is split on the right-hand side, you will—" But he did not finish the sentence, for a bullet from Whitson's revolver crushed through his brain, and he tumbled forward on his face into the fire.

It was only after tremendous difficulty that Whitson and Langley succeeded in escaping from the mountains. However, on the evening of the third day after their adventure in the cave, they came in sight of the police camp. Whitson sat down on a stone, and motioned his companion to do the same.

"See here, sonny," he said, "I want to have a short talk with you. I am a bit cross with you as the cause of my having been sucked in by that

d—d murdering old walrus. You ought to know
the inhabitants of this country better than a simple
stranger like me, and so I took your lead. Now,
another thing: you nearly bust us both by your
blasted foolishness in going to sleep that day; but
let that pass, because perhaps it would have been
worse if we had not been put on our guard; not
but that it would take a d—d smart cannibal to eat
Hiram Whitson. But this is what I am coming
to: you, my boy, are a darned sight too fond of
hearing your own tongue clack. Now, take a
warning from me, and don't let a word of what
has happened since we left camp for Pietermaritzburg pass your lips. I did all the shooting, and
I 'm not a bit ashamed of it; but, by the eternal
God, if you open your lips to a soul, I 'll shoot you
like a dog or a cannibal! Remember that, sonny,
and say it quietly over to yourself the first time you
feel that you want to blab. Now, shake hands."

This was probably the longest speech that Whitson had ever made.

About two years after the events narrated,
Whitson took his discharge and returned to Amer-
ica. He left behind him a sealed packet addressed
to his commanding officer, and which was not to
be delivered for twelve months after his departure.

Owing, however, to a strange combination of
fortuitous circumstances, this packet never reached
its proper destination; its wrapper, bearing the address, having been scorched off in a fire which took
place in the house where it was left.

Many people have heard or read of the cannibals of Natal, who turned large tracts of country into a shambles in the early part of this century, after Tshaka's impis had swept off all the cattle, and then kept the miserable people continually on the move so that they were unable to cultivate. One Umdava originated the practice of eating human flesh. Gathering together the fragments of four scattered tribes, he trained them to hunt human beings as others hunted game. This gang was a greater scourge to the country surrounding the present site of Pietermaritzburg than even Tshaka's murdering hordes. It was broken up in or about the year 1824, when the Europeans first came to the country, and the remnants of many scattered tribes returned and settled under their protection.

All this is history with which most people in South Africa are familiar, but many do not know that some of the cannibals fled to Basutoland, where, among almost inaccessible mountains, they carried on their horrible practices for many years.

It is a well-known fact that when men once surrender themselves to any unnatural and brutal vice, the gratification of the abnormal instinct thus acquired becomes the most imperative need of their nature. The Falkland Islands case, as bearing specially upon the foregoing narrative, may be mentioned. Some convicts escaped from the Falkland Island convict station, and succeeded in reaching the coast of Patagonia. They then endeavored to make their way to Montevideo, but having to keep along the shore so as to avoid the natives, who would have killed them had they ventured inland, were easily intercepted by the government cutter, which was always despatched in cases of the kind to head off fugitives upon their only possible course. Of the party only one man was found alive. In their dreadful need the men had cast lots as to who should be killed and eaten by the others, and this went on until only the one man remained. His sufferings had been so horrible that he was let off any further punishment, and simply brought back to the island to complete the term of his sentence. Some months after, this man induced another to escape with him in a boat, and, when the boat was overtaken, it was found he had killed his companion for the purpose of eating the latter's flesh. This was apparent from the fact that the supply of food which the fugitives had taken with them was not exhausted.

MARY MUSGRAVE

ANONYMOUS

MARY MUSGRAVE

"NINE carats ef it 's a blessed one."
"Scale 'im, an' ye 'll find he 's a half better.
Clear es a bottle o' gin, an' flawless es the pope!
Tommy Dartmoor, ye 're in luck, s' welp me never
ef ye ain't, an' that 's a brilliant yer can show the
polis an' not get time fer."

Tommy Dartmoor, who owed his surname to a
crown establishment within the restraining walls
of which he had once enjoyed a temporary resi-
dence, growled out a recommendation to "stow
that," and then added, "Boys, we 'll wet this.
Trek to Werstein's."

Forthwith a crowd of dirty, tanned diggers
turned their heads in the direction of Gustav
Werstein's American Bar, and walked toward it as
briskly as the heat and their weariness would ad-
mit of. The Israelite saw them coming, straightened himself out of the half-doze in which he had
passed the baking afternoon, stopped down the
tobacco in the porcelain bowl of his long-stemmed
pipe with stumpy forefinger, and, twisting a cork
off his corkscrew, stood in readiness.

"Name yer pizons, boys, an' get outside 'em,
wishin' all good luck to R'yal Straight; R'yal

Straight bein' the name o' this yer stone given by
Thomas D. Hesquire, original diskiverer an' present perprietor."

The orders were given,—bass at five shillings a
bottle, champagne (née gooseberry) at five pounds,
Cape smoke at two shillings per two fingers,—and,
at a given signal, there was an inarticulate roar
from dusty throats, an inversion of tumblers over
thirsty mouths, and a second inversion over the
ground to show that all the contents had disappeared.

Satan, the one cat and only domestic pet of the
camp, saw that there was a general treat going on,
and bustling up for his drink took a can of con-
densed milk at six shillings. Other diggers came
trooping in as the news spread, and Tommy Dartmoor, who was rapidly becoming mellow, for he
drank half a tumbler of raw whisky with every
one who nodded to him, stood them refreshments
galore, while the greasy Jew began to see visions
of his adopted fatherland in the near distance.

So the Kaffirs, except those who had supplies of
their own, kept sober and peaceful, while the
higher order of the human race at Big Stone Hole,
after the manner of their kind, began to squabble.
It was natural for them to do so, perhaps, for the
weather was hot, and the liquors, for the most
part, more so ; and under these circumstances men
do not always cast about them long for a casus
belli. One or two minor brawls opened the ball,
and Herr Gustav, scenting battle in the air, drew

from a locker a card, which he balanced against
the bottles on a shelf above his head. It read
thus :

GENTS IS REKESTED TO SHOOT
CLEAR OF THE BARR-KEP.
BROKIN GLAS MAY BE PADE FOR
AT COST PRISE.

and had been written for the German by a gentleman who had had some experience in Forty Rod
Gulch, Nevada. The action elicited a contemp-
tuous laugh from one or two of the new hands, but
the oldsters began shifting sundry articles which
depended from their belts into positions from
which they might be handled at the shortest notice ;
and the black cat, more wise than any of them,
having drunk his fill, stalked solemnly out into the
security of the darkness.

The sun went down,—went out with a click,
some one declared,—and, as no twilight interposed
between daylight and darkness in the country
which Big Stone Hole ornamented, Herr Gustav
lit his two paraffin-lamps. Neither boasted of
more than a one-inch wick, and, as their glasses
were extremely smoky, the illumination was not
brilliant ; but it sufficed to show the flushed, angry
faces of a couple of men standing in the centre
of the room, with all the others clustered round,
watching eagerly. One was the Scholar. The other
was a burly giant, whose missing left little finger
caused him to be nicknamed the Cripple. About

what they had originally fallen out was not clear
to any one, to themselves least of all. As the case
stood when the second lamp was lit, Scholar had
called Cripple a something-or-othered liar, and
Cripple, who was not inventive, had retorted by
stigmatising Scholar as another. Further recrimi-
nations followed, and their pistols were drawn;
but as the audience had a strong objection to in-
discriminate shooting, by which it was not likely to
benefit, the belligerents were seized. No one was
unsportsmanlike enough to wish to stop the fight,
and Jockey Bill, giving voice to the general wish
of the meeting, proposed that the gents be fixed
up agin' a couple o' posts outside, where they
might let daylight into each other without lead-
poisoning casual spectators.

The motion was acted on, and after rectifying a
slight omission on the Cripple's part—he had forgotten to put caps on the nipples of his revolver—
the pair of them were seated upon upturned barrels
some ten yards apart, each with a lamp at his feet,
and told to begin when they saw fit to do so. The
swarthy, bearded diggers grouped themselves on
either side, and the cat, emerging from his retreat,
scrambled on to the shoulder of one of them, fully
as curious as the rest to "see the shootin'." It
was a weird sight,—dust, scorched grass, empty
tins, rude hovels, piles of debris, African moonlight,—yet, except, perhaps, in the eyes of the newest comers, there was nothing strange in it. The
others were too wrapped up in what was going to

take place to see anything quaint in their every-day
surroundings. There was no theatre in the camp.
The little impromptu drama riveted all attention.

But before the duel commenced, a galloping
horse, which had approached over the grassy veldt
unnoticed during the excitement, drew up with a
crash between the two combatants, and its rider,
raising his hand to command attention, cried:

" Boys, there 's a white woman comin'!"

"A white woman!" was chorused in various
tones of disbelief. "What, here? White woman
comin' here, Dan?"

And then some one inquired if she was a Boer.

" Boer—no," replied Dan; " English—English
as I am; leastways Englisher, bein' Amurrican-
born myself. Overtook her et Hottentot Drift.
Thort I 'd spur on an' tell yer. We 'd do wi' a
clean-up, some on us."

Dan spoke indistinctly, as a bullet had lately
disarranged some of his teeth; but his words had
a wonderful effect.

Each man began instinctively to tidy himself.
The would-be duellists, forgetting their quarrel,
stuck the revolvers in their belts and followed the
general example. The Cripple hied him to the
store, and after breaking down the door abstracted
the only blacking-brush in the camp,—putting
down a sovereign on the counter in exchange for
it,—and set to polishing his high boots as if a fortune depended on their brightness. The Scholar
bought Herr Gustav's white shirt for a fiver, threat-

ening to murder its owner if he did not render it
up. And Partridge, a good man from Norfolk,
with a regrettable weakness for shooting other
people's game, induced a friend to denude him of
his flowing locks by means of a clasp-knife and a
hunk of wood, as no scissors were procurable.

The wardrobes of Big Stone Hole were stocked
more with a view to strict utility than variety or
ornamentation, and the slender resources of the
store utterly gave out under the sudden strain that
was put upon them. In every direction grimy,
unkempt men might be seen attempting to beautify themselves. Here was one enduring agonies
from a razor that would scarcely whittle a stick;
here another recalling the feel of a cake of soap;
there a great fellow pulling faces as he struggled
to get the teeth of a comb into his shock of hair;
there another brushing the clay from his moleskin
trousers with a tuft of stiff grass.

It seemed to these men ages since they had last
seen a woman in the flesh,—Kaffir women don't
count; they are not women, merely Kaffirs,—and,
with the natural instinct of males of every species,
they set about pluming their feathers.

These operations, though speedy as might be,
were necessarily prolonged, for most of the men required several buckets of water over the head before they felt fit for such unaccustomed exercises,
and they were scarcely finished before the creak-
ing of wheels and the cries of the voorlooper as
he urged his oxen announced that the wagon was

within earshot. Up it came, the great tilt gleaming white in the moonlight, and every eye was fixed
expectantly on the dark chasm within. The driver,
puffed up with his own importance, cracked his
long whip and deigned not to notice the men
whom he usually greeted with a friendly hail, and
the Hottentot boy ahead, imitating his master,
vouchsafed no explanation. With more deathly
slowness than usual did the lumbering vehicle
crawl along until the tired cattle pulled up before
the door of the American Bar. Then there was a
rush and a bit of a scuffle for the honour of hand-
ing the woman out. The Cripple was the fortunate man, and, after assisting her to the ground,
waved his tattered hat toward the gleaming open
doorway. But he did not speak. Words were
beyond him. Indeed, the diggers, who were none
of them particularly remarkable for taciturnity as
a general thing, seemed, with one exception, to be
stricken dumb. But the Scholar proved himself
equal to the occasion, and with courtly phrase bade
the new-comer welcome to the camp. He had
always been a popular man among women in his
palmier days, though openly holding rather a poor
opinion of them; and as the one before him now
was neat of speech and comely of form, he was
not at all averse to enjoying her society and conversation.

" I should be much obliged if you would direct
me to a hotel," she said, after taking a look around
the cheap gaudiness of the saloon.

"I 'm sorry to say that we have no hotel here as yet, Miss—er—?"

"Musgrave. Miss Mary Musgrave"—with a little bow. "But I heard that a German had started a hotel here."

"No; there is nothing but this. That"—pointing to Herr Gustav, who was regarding the newcomer with an evil eye—"that is the German."

Miss Musgrave appeared distressed.

"Then where can I go?" she asked. "Are there any lodgings to be had?"

"The lady may have my place," chorused three eager voices, and every man in the room repeated the offer.

She thanked them with a pretty smile and one comprehensive bow, and looked up at the Scholar for help.

"I would offer you my hut if it were not such a wretched one. But, as it is, I should advise you to take this man's"—and he pointed to Tommy Dartmoor.

"Why, mine 's twenty carats better than hisn!" exclaimed the Cripple.

"And mine better 'n either," growled Dan.

"Mine 's the best of the lot."

"No, it is n't; mine is," yelled others, till there was a general roar, which caused Miss Musgrave to look frightened and shrink nearer to the Scholar, and that gentleman to raise his hand for silence.

"Look here," said he, "we 'll pick out the

twelve best, and their owners can cut with one
another from a pack of cards."

After some discussion twelve were settled upon,
but the number was immediately raised to thirteen
to prevent Jockey Bill disgracing the camp by
shooting before a lady. A pack of cards was
placed on the bar, and each man chose one, holding his selection face downward till all were ready.
Then the Scholar said, " Turn," and there were exhibited five aces, two kings, a queen, three knaves,
and two smaller cards. This was awkward, to say
the least of it, and, while sarcastic laughter rippled
among the spectators, there was an instinctive
movement of right hands toward the back of the
belt on the part of each of the thirteen.

But the Scholar's voice, full of remonstrance,
said, " Boys, you 're being looked at," and there
was a regretful sigh or two, but no bloodshed.

Miss Musgrave gazed inquiringly from one to
another, and the Scholar, laying his hand on her
arm, whispered something in her ear. She smiled,
whispered back, and was answered, and then, strip-
ping off a pair of well-fitting fawn gloves, she took
the cards in a pretty little white hand, and dealt
out one to each of the competitors with charming
clumsiness.

" Ain't touched a keard afore, bless her," whispered Euchre Buck, giving his neighbour Dan a
nudge in the ribs to call attention to this wonderful piece of girlish innocence. " Square a deal es
George Washington mought ha' made." Then, as

the greasy pasteboards were turned up, and his neighbour was handed the ace of clubs, he raised his voice and yelled out, " Bully for you, Dan! Cut away an' clar yer cabin out."

Away scampered Dan out into the darkness, with the rest of the crew at his heels. Their home comforts were very small, poor fellows; but each gave of his best, though the gifts were often incongruous enough. In half an hour the cabin was fitted out with a small cracked looking-glass, two combs, an old hair-brush,—still wet from the wash,—a pail, a frying-pan, three kettles, two three-legged stools, and so many blankets that some were requisitioned to carpet the floor. The whole crowd accompanied Miss Musgrave to her door and gave her a cheer by way of good-night. She bowed to them, smiling her thanks, and looking, as they thought, entrancingly lovely as she stood there, with the pale moonbeams falling full on her.

Then she turned to go in, but as Euchre Buck stepped forward with an admonishing cough, she waited and looked round at him.

" Miss," said he, holding out a big revolver in his hard fist, " you take this yer gun, an' ef any one whistles, or otherwise disturbs you, let a hole into him straight away, an' we 'll see him buried decent."

But Miss Musgrave courteously, and with profuse thanks, refused the offer, and, saying that she had perfect confidence in all who were around her, gave Euchre Buck a bewitching smile, went inside, and closed the door after her.

Then the diggers returned to Gustav Werstein's American Bar and discussed the new arrival.

"I known Noomarket an' Hascot an' Hepsom, an' all the places where swells goes in England," said Jockey Bill, enthusiastically; "but never one come there as pretty as she, stop my license if ther' did."

"Grand eyes, hain't she?" said Tommy Dartmoor. "Regular fust-water 'uns. Here's to 'em!"

"And—a—hoof! See it peep below her gownd. S' welp me ef it wer' es big es my 'bacca-box!"

"An' 'er close, gentlemen! Made to measure, every thread on 'em, I allow."

"She's a lady, boys," exclaimed he who had offered to see after a funeral, "a reg'lar slap-up, high-toned, blow-yer-eyes-don't-touch-me lady; an' as she sees fit to do the civil to this fellar"—striking himself on the chest—"he's just going to drop his professional name, an' arsk yer to call him Mister Samuel K. Gregson, Esquire. Play on that."

Next morning the inhabitants of Big Stone Hole were startled by reading this announcement outside the cabin which Dan had resigned to Miss Musgrave:

SINGING AND MUSIC TAUGHT.
LITERARY WORK DONE.

It was printed on a card, which was affixed to the door by means of a drawing-pin, and from within came the sound of a contralto voice singing to a guitar accompaniment. One by one the male residents of Big Stone Hole drew near to that iron-roofed hut and stopped to listen; but after commenting on the innovation in gleeful whispers—for guitar had never twanged in that part of Africa before—they moved on to their work. No consideration could cause them to neglect that. They might fritter away the dull, rough gems when they had found them, but the lust of handling diamonds once was the strongest passion they knew. And so the day's toil was not curtailed; but at the conclusion Miss Musgrave had an application for instruction in music from every man in the camp, with one exception. This one defaulter was Euchre Buck. He owned to having no ear for music—thereby exhibiting more honesty than many of the others—and confessed to knowing only two tunes, one of which was "Hail Columbia," and the other—was n't; and so he said he wanted some "literary work done." He proposed to Miss Musgrave that she should write a history of his life at half a guinea a page, thereby—cute Yankee that he was—thinking to appropriate the whole of her time.

But embarrassed by all these calls upon her, and obviously unable to satisfy each of them, Miss Musgrave turned for help to the Scholar, whom she appeared to regard as her special adviser; and he, promising a solution of the difficulty in half an hour, drew off the whole crowd to the American Bar, where the question was thrashed out in all its points.

It was clearly evident that Miss Musgrave could not surrender to each individual the whole of her evening, even if any one had been willing to let his neighbour monopolise it, which no one was; and therefore it was necessary to formulate some scheme by which her talents might be distributed over a larger area. But what the scheme should be was not settled all in a minute. One man wanted to hear her sing, another to hear her talk, another was willing to give five pounds an hour for the privilege of talking to her. After a lengthened discussion, which was excited throughout, and at times verged on the warlike, it was decided to effect a compromise—subject, of course, to Miss Musgrave's inclinations; and a deputation was sent to learn her views on the subject.

There was no assembly-room in the place, excepting Werstein's saloon,—which, of course, was not available for such a purpose,—and so it was proposed to her, with much humility, that she should take up her position in the evenings on a chair outside her hut, and there discourse such vocal and instrumental music as she saw fit, interlarding the same with friendly conversation. What was she to talk about? Anything—absolutely anything. They did n't mind what it was, so long as they heard her voice. Five shillings, the committee had decided, was to be paid by every man who came within earshot. And any one who wanted a free list was requested to argue the matter out with Euchre Buck.

This call upon her powers seemed to take Miss Musgrave aback.

"I have never sung in public," she pleaded, rather nervously. "Indeed, my voice is not good enough for it; really it is n't. Only I thought I could teach a little perhaps, and that is why I came here. You see, mother is an invalid, and we were so very poor that—"

"Miss," broke in Jockey Bill, "call it ten bob a 'ead, an' just 'um to us."

"Oh no, Mr. William, it was not the money that I thought about; indeed, five shillings would be far too much. But if you think that I should be able to amuse you at all, I would do my very best—believe me, I would."

"Miss," growled Dan, with a clumsy endeavour to chase away her diffidence, "all we asks is fer you to sit near us fer a spell. Ef you sings or plays, we 'd be proud; ef you just looks an' talks, we 'd be pleased."

So in the end Miss Musgrave yielded to the wishes of the community, and the nightly conclave in the American Bar became so much a thing of the past that Gustav Werstein was heard to threaten another emigration. The songs were to the diggers new, and yet not new. There was nothing of the music-hall type about them; they were nearly all old-fashioned ditties. She sang to them of "Barbara Allen" and "Sally in our Alley"; she gave them "Cheer, Boys, Cheer," and called for a chorus; she sang "The Message," "The Arrow

and the Song"; and she brought back memories
of other days when Africa was to them a mere
geographical expression—of days when that something had not happened which had sent them away
from home.

Sunday came, the fifth day after her arrival, and
it differed from the usual Sabbath of Big Stone
Hole. Sunday had been observed before by the
biggest drinking bout of the week, and a summary
settlement of the previous six days' disputes.
Now, to the huge surprise of the Kaffirs, and to
the still greater surprise of themselves, these dia-
mond-diggers sang hymns at intervals during the
day, and refrained from indulging in the orthodox
carouse till after Miss Musgrave had retired for the
night. It was a wonderful change.

During the next week a fall of earth took place
in Tommy Dartmoor's claim. Two Kaffirs were
killed; and when the proprietor himself was ex-
tricated from the debris of blue clay which held
him down, he was found to have a broken arm,
besides other serious injuries.

"Don't let on to her," he managed to gasp out
to his rescuers, wishing to spare Miss Musgrave's
nerves a shock.

But she saw the men bearing him to his hut,
joined them, and insisted on being installed as sole
nurse forthwith.

Twenty other men would willingly have broken
an arm for such a reward; and the recklessness
displayed during the next few days was something

awful. But she saw that too,—little escaped those big blue eyes,—and, ascribing it to drink, gave a pretty strong lecture on the bibulous habits of Big Stone Hole, at her next concert.

There was an earnest meeting in the American Bar that night, at which the following motion was put and carried unanimously: " On and after this date, any drunken man is liable to be shot at sight, unless his friends can prove that he has dug over three carats of diamonds during the day." And then, like other reformers, they went on to more sweeping measures: " Only knife-fighting to take place in the camp. All disputes with pistols, unless of a very pressing nature, to be settled out of earshot of Dan's house." There were even some hints of appointing a closing-time for the saloon —" it would make the place so much more like home." But the promoter eventually withdrew his suggestion, as it was justly felt that such a motion would interfere with the liberty of the subject too much. But a storm of cheers burst forth when it was proposed to transfer the diamond-safe from Werstein's keeping to a corner of the new goddess's shrine.

Even Satan, the cat, joined in the general adoration, and, more favoured than the rest, enjoyed at times a chaste salute from Miss Musgrave's ripe-red lips.

Never, in so short a space of time, had a community been more changed for the better than was that of Big Stone Hole. Never had woman's humanising influence made itself more clearly felt. The azure cloud of blasphemy that hung over the workings and the rest of the camp was replaced again by the normal dust. Each man tried to beautify the inside of his shanty to the best of his means and ideas, for there was no knowing when the only "she" would take it into her pretty, capricious head to pay a call. In this latter line the Scholar had a decided pull. Education had taught him taste; necessity, handiness; and by aid of the two he transformed his rude dwelling into something approaching the rooms in which he used to dawdle away the happy hours, time ago. It was partly drawing-room, partly curiosity-shop. Cups, saucers, and spoons appeared as if by magicians' call, and one blazing afternoon the news flashed round the diamond-pits that Miss Musgrave was "taking afternoon tea with the Scholar." But when the Scholar saw the dismay his simple act had spread around him, he dissipated it with a kindly laugh and a few reassuring words.

"Don't mind me, boys. I was only doing the civil in a purely platonic manner. Miss Musgrave is nothing to me, nor am I anything to her. Heaven forbid! I 'm too hard a bargain for any girl. If any one of you marries her I 'll act as his best man if he asks me to, and wish him every felicity without a thought of regret."

"Bully for the Scholar!" yelled the delighted crowd; and Miss Musgrave's smiles were more sought after than ever.

So things went on day after day, week after week, till Miss Musgrave became little short of an autocratic empress.   But still she showed no signs of taking unto herself a consort; she kept all men at a cousinly distance, and those who felt intimate enough to address her as " Miss Mary " accounted themselves uncommonly fortunate.   Thus the little machine of state worked perfectly harmoniously, and Big Stone Hole was as steady and prosperous a settlement as need be.

Had these diggers refreshed their minds by looking back for historical parallels, they might have been prepared in some degree for Miss Musgrave's exit from among them, but as none of them indulged in such retrospections the manner of it took the camp somewhat by surprise.

It was first discovered in this wise.   Work was over for the day.   The Kaffirs had been searched and had returned to their kraal.   Pipes were being lit after the evening meal, and a picturesque assembly was grouping itself in an expectant semicircle on the sun-baked turf in front of Miss Musgrave's dwelling.   She was usually outside to welcome the first comers, and her absence naturally formed the staple topic of conversation.   Digger after digger arrived, threw himself down, and joined in the general wonderment as to why Miss Mary was n't there, and at last some one hazarded a suggestion that she " must be asleep."   There was a general epidemic of noisy coughing for a full minute, and then silence for another, but no sound from within the hut.

" Perhaps she 's ill," was the next surmise.

After the etiquette to be followed had been strictly discussed, and a rigid course of procedure set down, the Scholar got up and knocked at the door. He received no answer, and so knocked again—knocked several times, in fact, and then rattled the handle vigorously, but without result.

" Better open it," said a voice.

And he did so; and after looking inside, announced:

" She 's not there."

At this moment Dan came up.

" My ole mar' 's gone," he said; " an' she ain't stampeded, neither, but was stole. Tote-rope 's been untied, an' saddle an' bridle took as well."

There was uncomfortable silence, which the Scholar broke by a low, long-drawn whistle.

" Boys," said he, " let 's look inside the safe."

The three men who held the keys brought them up, the bolts were shot, and the massive door swung back. There was every man's little sack with his name on it; but somehow or other the sacks looked limper than of yore. Each one was eagerly clutched and examined, and many a groan and not a few curses went up on the still night air as it was found that every sack save Dan's had been relieved of the more valuable part of its contents.

So much heart-breaking labour under the burning sun thrown away for nothing; the dreary work to commence afresh, almost from the beginning! Had the thief been any ordinary one, the denunciation would have been unbounded; but no one lifted his tongue very loudly against Mary Musgrave. Yet mounted men were despatched on the three trails to bring back the booty if possible, and the rest moved dejectedly toward their old club. The greasy Jew did not attempt to conceal his exultation. He served his customers with his wicked old face glowing with smiles, and when a moment's breathing-time came he observed:

"We all 'az our leetle surbrizes in dis wairld, an' I most confaiss I am asdonished myself to lairn dat Mess Mosgrave is a thief—" But here a crashing among the glassware announced that Tommy Dartmoor had begun shooting with his left hand, and Herr Gustav spluttered out from behind the fingers he held before his face, "Ach Gott! I say nozzing more!"

GREGORIO

BY

ARTHUR HEMINGWAY

GREGORIO

BY 'ARTHUR HEMINGWAY

I

AT THE PARADISO

THE Café Paradiso was full of people, for the inhabitants of Alexandria had dined, and the opera season was over. The seats at every table were occupied, and the fumes of smoke from a hundred cigars partly hid the ladies of the orchestra. As the waiters pushed aside the swing-doors of the buffet and staggered into the salon with whisky, absinthe, and coffee, the click of billiard-balls was heard. The windows facing the sea were wide open, for the heat was intense, and the murmur of the waves mingled with the plaintive voices of the violins.

Seated by a table at the far end of the hall, Gregorio Livadas hummed softly an accompaniment to Suppé's " Poète et Paysan," puffing from time to time a cloudlet of blue smoke from his mouth. When the music ceased he joined in the applause, leaning back happily in his chair as the musicians prepared to repeat the last movement. Meanwhile his eyes wandered idly over the faces of his neighbours.

When the last chord was struck he saw the women hurry down from the platform and rush toward the tables where their acquaintances sat. He heard them demand beer and coffee, and they drank eagerly, for fiddling in that heat was thirsty work. He watched the weary waiters hastening from table to table, and he heard the voices around him grow more animated and the laughter more frequent. One man was fastening a spray of flowers on the ample bosom of the flautiste, while another sipped the brown lager from the glass of the big drum, and the old wife of the conductor left her triangle and cymbals to beg some roses from an Arab flower-girl. Truly the world was enjoying itself, and Gregorio smiled dreamily, for the sight of so much gaiety pleased him. He wished one of the women would come and talk to him; he would have liked to chat with the fair-haired girl who played the first violin so well. He began to wonder why she preferred that ugly Englishman with his red face and bald head. He caught snatches of their conversation. Bah! how uninteresting it was! for they could barely understand each other. What pleasure did she find in listening to his bad French? and in her native Hungarian he could not even say, " I love." Why had she not come to him, Gregorio Livadas, who could talk to her well and would not mumble like an idiot and look red and uncomfortable! Then he saw she was drinking champagne, and he sighed. Ah, yes, these English were rich, and women only cared for money; they were unable to give up their luxuries for the sake of a man.

But at this thought Gregorio blushed a little. After all, there was one woman—the only woman he ought to think of—who was not afraid of hardship for the sake of her husband. He tried to excuse himself by arguing that the music had excited him; but he felt a little ashamed, and as a sop to his not yet quite murdered conscience got up and left the café.

When he turned into the Place Mehemet Ali he remembered suddenly that he had wasted his evening. It was ten o'clock, too late to set about the business he had intended. He was angry with himself now as well as ashamed. He wandered up and down the square, looking at the statue of the great khedive, silhouetted against the moonlight, and cursed at his misfortunes.

Why should he, Gregorio Livadas, be in need of money? He had worked hard, but without success. He could have borne his ill luck had he alone been the sufferer, but he must consider his child—and, of course, his wife too. He was really fond of his wife in a way. But he smiled proudly as he thought of his son, for whom he schemed out a great future. He and Xantippe would train the boy so carefully that he would grow up to be a great man, and, what was more, a rich man. How they would laugh, all three, as they sat in the splendid cafés over their wine, at the hardships the father had endured! Still he must not forget

the present, and he sorely needed money. He
would go to Amos again. Amos was a rich man,
very rich, and a filthy Jew. Amos could easily
spare him some money and renew the last loan.
He was going to be successful now and would be
able to pay good interest. What better investment
could Amos have? Surely none. He was going
to set up a café with the money at Tanta, or Zaga-
zig, or even Benhur,—yes, Benhur was the best,—
where there were few competitors. Then he
would make a fortune, as other Greeks had done,
and Amos would be paid in full. He was not ex-
travagant, no; he had the business instincts of his
race. Half these rich merchants of Alexandria
had begun as he would begin; he would succeed
as they had succeeded. The future was really
hopeful, if he could only borrow a little capital.

With these thoughts surging through his brain
Gregorio paced up and down the pavements.
At last he turned into the Rue des Sœurs and
started slowly toward his home.

This street, the sink of Alexandria, was at its
gayest. The cafés where cheap liquor is sold
were crowded. Soldiers and sailors, natives and
the riffraff of half a dozen nations, jostled one
another. The twanging of guitars and the tinkling
of pianos was heard from every house. Women,
underclothed and overpainted, leaned from the
upper windows and made frequent sallies into the
street to capture their prey. Loud voices sang
lusty English choruses and French chansonnettes,

and Neapolitan songs tried to assert themselves whenever the uproar ceased for a moment. Every one talked his, or her, own tongue, and gesture filled in the gaps when words were wanting. All seemed determined to degrade themselves as much as possible, and nearly every one seemed supremely happy.

Occasionally there was a fight, and knives were used with unerring skill; but the mounted police who patrolled the streets, though overtaxed, managed to preserve a certain amount of order.

Gregorio took very little notice of the scenes through which he passed. He knew every inch and corner of the quarter that had been his home for years, and was familiar with most of its inhabitants. He sighed a little as he thought of the money being lost and won in the stuffy ill-lighted rooms at the back of the houses, shut out from view of the authorities. Like most of his race, he was fond of the excitement of gambling. But of what use were regrets and sighs? he had no money, and must needs go home. It was vain to try and borrow or to ask credit for his losses: in these gambling hells what is lost must be immediately paid, for tempers are inflamed by drink and knives are worn at each player's belt.

But he sighed, none the less, at the hard necessity that compelled him to pass down the street without once entering the doors of a tavern. It was very hot, and he had smoked many cigarettes. He would have been glad to call for a drink. The tavern-keepers, though they were his friends, expected to be paid. One or two women beckoned to him, who would have willingly offered him wine, but he was proud enough to ignore them.

He became more moody and dejected as he went along, silent and sober amid so much revelry. When he reached his house he saw a drunken man lying on the threshold asleep. He stooped to look into his face and recognised an Englishman, the foreman of some tramp in the harbour. He kicked the recumbent form testily as he strode over it.

"These English, what beasts they are!" he growled, "and I—I have not a piastre for a single glass of wine."

II

CONCERNING A DEBT

GREGORIO found, on entering his house, that his wife was already in bed. He went into the tiny kitchen and saw a plate of macaroni ready for his supper. He tried to eat some, but it stuck in his throat. He took a bottle of cheap Cretan wine from a shelf and drank from it; but the wine was sour, and he spat it from his mouth with a curse.

Taking up the lamp, he went into the bedroom. His wife was fast asleep with the boy in her arms. For a moment a smile flickered round Gregorio's mouth as he looked at them. Then he took off his boots and his coat, blew out the lamp, and lay beside them. He was very tired after his long tramp in the hot streets, but he could not sleep. Angrily he tossed from side to side and closed his eyes tightly; but it was no good, sleep would not come.

At midnight he heard the call to prayer chanted from the minaret of a tiny mosque in the neighbourhood. The muezzin's voice irritated him. He did not wish to pray, and he did want to sleep. He swore that it was insanity for these fools of Mohammedans to declare that prayer was better than sleep.

Then the thoughts that had agitated him during the walk returned to him. The Rue des Sœurs was still noisy with merry-makers, and it seemed to him that if he could only join them he would be happy. But he had no money, and one can do nothing without money!

Then there came back to him the face of the Englishman he had seen talking to the violinist of the Paradiso. He hated the man because he was ugly and rich. These English were all rich, and yet they seemed to him a miserable race, mere ignorant bullies. He remembered how often he had come to the help of the English travellers who filled Egypt. Why had he, he asked himself, for the sake of a miserable reward, prevented them being cheated, when he, with all his talents, was condemned to starve? Even his child, he thought, would grow to hate him if he remained poor. He must get money. Amos would have to lend him some. The Jews were unpopular among the

Greeks; it were wise to keep on good terms with them, as Amos would find out.

At last he fell asleep.

In the morning his troubles began again. There was no coffee, and only a little Arab bread, and when that was done they must starve if they could not get some money. Gregorio tore off a bit of bread and ate it slowly, looking at his wife, who sat weeping beside him.

" I shall go to Amos," he said, firmly.

" Ah, yes, to Amos," Xantippe answered, quietly; " but it will be no good."

" Why no good? "

" Because you owe him money, and he will give you no more till he is paid."

" But we cannot pay him. He must let us have some. If not—" and Gregorio raised his hand threateningly.

His wife smiled sadly and kissed him.

" You will not frighten Amos, my love. When I told him the child had been ill, he only laughed."

" When was that? "

" Yesterday."

" Then he has been here? "

" He came last night to ask for his money. I told him we had none, and he laughed and said we must get some. He told me I might get some if I cared to. He said I could make, oh, so much! "

Gregorio scowled savagely. " The filthy Jew! he said that? Never, never, never!"

"But we must get some money," the woman sobbed, "if only for our son's sake, Gregorio. But not that way?"

"No, not that way," he replied, savagely.

"When shall you go to him?"

"Now."

And taking up his hat he rushed into the street. He was terribly angry, not so much at the purport of the Jew's speech as at the man who made it. He loathed the Jews, and felt insulted when spoken to by one; it was a terrible matter to ask this man for help, but it was intolerable that his wife should suffer insult. And yet the child must be fed. Yes, she had said that, and it was true. They must make sacrifices for the child.

He soon reached the Jew's house, and was shown by a richly clad servant into the room where Amos sat. Amos was an old man, tall and strong, with a long bushy beard, in which his fingers continually played; and his eyes were sharp and brilliant and restless, a strange contrast to his stately bearing and measured movements. He rose from his cushions as Gregorio entered, and saluted him courteously, motioning him to a seat. Then, having resettled himself, he clapped his hands together smartly and ordered the servant who answered the summons to bring in coffee and pipes.

Gregorio was rather overawed at the luxury he saw around him, and he felt the stern-looking, polite old man would be a difficult person to deal with. As he puffed at his tube he considered carefully what words he should use.

For some time neither spoke, but Amos was the first to break the silence.

" You heard I was at your house last night, and so have come at once to pay me? "

" Yes, I heard you were at my house and that you wanted to be paid. You are a rich man, and I am poor."

" Nay, I am not rich; they lie who say I am rich."

" It is twenty pounds I owe you, is it not? "

" Yes, twenty pounds. It is a large sum, and I have dealt generously with you. I am now in need of it myself."

" I am a poor man."

" You have not the money, eh, my friend? "

" I have not the money. But I will pay you if you will lend me some more. I shall be successful now; only twenty pounds more."

Amos appeared unmoved at the tremor in Gregorio's voice. His eyes rested coldly on the face of his client, while the unfortunate Greek continued to speak rapidly of his troubles and hopes. He smiled sarcastically as Gregorio spoke of the certainty of making his fortune at Benhur, and remained quite unmoved at the story of the sufferings of a woman and child from hunger and want.

" Your wife is beautiful," was all he answered when Gregorio paused for a moment. At these words, however, he half rose from his place and clinched his hands savagely. But he sank back again with the remembrance that a show of temper would not advance his cause.

"Very beautiful," he answered, chokingly; "would you see her starve?"

"She is not my wife," said Amos, quietly. Then he continued slowly, pausing at intervals to puff out a cloud of smoke from his mouth :

"You have owed me this money a long time. I want it, and I will have it. Even in Egypt there is law. You do not like us Jews, but the law will protect me as long as I am rich enough to buy justice. In three days you will pay me this money. I have been generous to you; now I will be generous no longer. If I am not paid I will take measures to recover my loss. You will sleep in the streets like the Arabs, my friend; but the weather is warm. It is early summer, so you will scarcely feel the exposure. In three days you will come and pay me."

"But how am I to get the money? If you would lend me only a few pounds I would repay you all I owe."

"Already you owe me more than you can pay. You can make money. You are married. These Christian women are worse than the Arabs; do I not see them as I come home in the evening from my business? It is not right to borrow and not repay. I need my money. How can I have my coffee and my pipe unless I have money?"

Gregorio listened with growing anger, and finally

rose from his seat and shook his fist in the old man's face.

"You shall be paid," he shouted, "you shall be paid!"

"Anger is useless, my friend."

And as Gregorio left the house Amos smiled and stroked his beard. "Truly," he thought, "these Christians hate us, but we have them in our power. It is pleasant to be hated and yet to know that it is to us they must cringe when they are in need; and it is very pleasant to refuse. My friend Gregorio is not happy now that he is struggling in my grasp."

As for Gregorio, he wandered away toward the harbour, kicking savagely at the refuse scattered along the pavement. He did not know how to set about earning the requisite sum. It was no good applying to the hotels or tourist agencies, for there were few visitors in the city and dragomen were therefore not needed.

His friends were too poor to help him, and the consul was unable to do much for him, there were so many poor Greeks who wanted help. Meanwhile there was no food at home and no drink; even the necessaries of life were lacking.

On arriving at his home he found his wife and child huddled in a corner crying for food. They ran toward him as he entered, but the hope in their faces quickly faded at sight of him.

"It 's no good," Gregorio growled; "Amos refuses to advance a piastre and says I must pay all I owe in three days."

" It is impossible to sleep when one is hungry," said Gregorio that night to his wife, who lay awake, weeping, beside him.

III

OF FAILURE AND A RESOLVE

GREGORIO's dreams, when he did sleep, were none of the pleasantest, and when he woke up, from time to time, he heard his wife weeping. In wondering what he should say to comfort her he fell asleep again, and sleeping was worse than lying awake. For in his dreams he saw Xantippe and his child starving and crying for food, and he was unable to help them in any way. He lived over again the long day he had spent tramping the streets of Alexandria searching for work. He saw the few tourists still left in the town fat and happy; he saw the porters of the hotels who had smiled on him pityingly and yet contemptuously; and he woke, after each representation of the crude comedy, hot and yet cold with perspiration, to feel the bed on which he lay shaking under the sobs of his wife.

When at last day dawned Gregorio raised himself with an oath, and swore to find food for his family and work for himself. The terrible debt he owed to Amos he swore should not trouble him, laughing at his wife's remonstrances. With the bright daylight had come a new courage, and,

hungry as he was, he felt able not only to satisfy
their hunger, but so skilfully to arrange matters
that they would never feel hungry again.   Yet it
was a terrible ordeal, that half-hour when the family should have sat down to a table laden with
food.   The poor wife cried, and he had to comfort her tears with promises, unsubstantial nutri-
ment indeed, and they could not satisfy the child,
who failed dismally to understand them.   Through
the green blinds came the noise of life and health
and merriment; curses too, sometimes, but only
the curses of the well fed, and therefore meaning-
less.   Aready the sun fell hot and indomitable on
all things; its long gold shadowy fingers crept into
the room, and the atmosphere at their touch became stifling.   Gregorio, swallowing his tears, tore
out into the street, shouting up the narrow stairway
hysterical words of hope.

How long and shadowless the street seemed!
Every house had its green blinds closely shut;
the wind that stirred the dust of the pavements was
hot and biting.   Gregorio clinched his hands and
strode rapidly onward.   What mattered it to him
that behind those green blinds women and men
slumbered in comparative comfort?   He had a
work to do, and by sunset must carry good tidings
to his little world.   For a time his heart was brave
as the dry wind scorched the tear upon his cheek.
"Surely," he thought, weaving his thoughts into a
fine marching rhythm, "the great God will help
me now, will help me now."

At midday, after he had tried, with that strange
Greek pertinacity that understands no refusals, all
the hotels and tourist agencies he had called at the
day before, he became weary and disconsolate.
The march had become a dirge; no longer it suggested happiness to be, but failure. An Englishman threw him a piastre, and he turned into a
café. Calling for a glass of wine, he flung himself
down on the wooden bench and tried to think. But
really logical thinking was impossible. For in spite
of the sorrow at his heart, the same bright dreams
of wealth and happiness came back to mock him.
The piastre he played with became gold, and he
felt the café contained no luxuries that he might
not command to be brought before him. But as
the effects of the red wine of Lebanon evaporated
he began to take a soberer though still cheerful view
of his position. It was only when the waiter carried off his piastre that he suddenly woke to fact
and knew himself once more a man with a wife and
child starving in Alexandria, an alien city for all its
wealthy colony of Greeks. A wave of pity swept
over him ; not so much for the woman was he sorry,
though he loved her too, but for the baby whose
future he had planned. He scowled savagely at
the inmates of the café, who only smiled quietly,
for they were used to poor Greeks who had drunk
away their last coin, and pushed past them into
the street.

There it was hotter than ever, and he met
scarcely any one. Every one who could be was

at home, or in the cool cafés; only Gregorio was
abroad.   He determined to make for the quay.
He knew that many ships put into the Alexandrian
waters, and there was often employment found for
those not too proud to work at lading and unload-
ing.   Quickly, and burning as the kempsin, he
hurried through the Rue des Sœurs, not daring to
look up at the house wherein he dwelt.   The
muffled sounds of voices and guitars from the far-
away interiors seemed to mock his footsteps as he
passed the wine-shops; and all the other houses
were silent and asleep.   At last he arrived on the
quay, and the black lines of the P. and O. stood
out firmly before him against the pitiless blue of
sea and sky.   He wandered over the hot stone
causeway, but found no one.   The revenue officers
were away, and not a labourer, not a sailor, was
visible.   Beyond the breakwater little tufts of sil-
very foam flashed on the rollers, and a solitary
steamer steered steadily for the horizon.   He
could see the Greek flag at her stern, and his eyes
filled with tears.   Ah, how little his friends in
Athens thought of the man who had come to find
fame and fortune in the far-off East!   He sat down
on the parapet and watched the vessel until she became a tiny speck on the horizon, and then he re-
commenced his search for work.   His heart was
braver for a moment because of its pangs; he
swore he would show these countrymen of his who
dwelt at home, and who in three days would see
the very ship he had been gazing at arrive in

Grecian waters, that he was still worthy of his country and his kinsfolk.

But resolutions were useless, tenacity of purpose was useless. For two long hours he wandered by the harbour, but met no one.

At last the sun fell behind the western waves, and the windows of the khedive's palace glowed like a hundred flaming eyes; the flags fell from the masts of the vessels; on the city side was a sudden silence, save for the melancholy voices of the muezzins; then the day died; the bright stars, suddenly piercing the heavens, mocked him with their brilliance and told him that his useless search for bread was over.

Gregorio went back slowly to his home. Already the Rue des Sœurs was crowded. The long street rang with music and laughter, and instead of blinds covering the windows merry women leaned upon the sills and laughed at the crowds below.

Gregorio, when he reached his house, would have liked to go straight to bed. But it was not to be, for as he entered the tiny room he heard his wife trying to persuade the hungry infant into sleep, and his footsteps disturbed her tears. He had to calm them as best he could, and as he soothed her he noticed the child had a crust in his hand which he gnawed half contentedly. At the same moment the dim blue figure of an Arab passed by the opposite wall, and had almost gained the door ere Gregorio found words.

"Who are you?"

"It is Ahmed," his wife answered, gently, placing her trembling hand upon his shoulder; "he too has children."

Gregorio scowled and muttered, "An Arab," and in that murmur none of the loathing was hidden that the pseudo-West bears for the East.

"The child was starving," said Ahmed. "I have saved the child; maybe some day I shall save the father." And Ahmed slipped away before Gregorio could answer him.

For a while neither he nor his wife spoke; they stood silent in the moonlight. At last Gregorio asked huskily, "Have you had food?"

"Not to-day," was the answer; and the sweet voice was almost discordant in its pathos as it continued, "nor drink, and but for Ahmed the boy had died."

Gregorio could not answer; there was a lump in his throat that blocked words, opening the gate for sobs. But he choked down his emotion with an effort and busied himself about the room. Xantippe sat watching him anxiously, smoothing with nervous fingers the covering of her son's bed.

As the night advanced the heat increased, and all that disturbed the silence of the room was the echo of the streets. Gregorio walked to the window and looked out. Below him he saw the jostling crowd of men and women. These people, he thought, were happy, and two miserables only dwelt in the city—his wife and himself. And whenever he asked himself what was the cause of his misery, the answer was ever the same—poverty. He glanced at his son, tossing uneasily in his bed ; he looked at his wife, pale and haggard in the moonlight; he remembered his own sufferings all day long in the hot cruel streets, and he spoke unsteadily :

" Xantippe? "

" Yes."

" I have thought over things."

" And I too."

" We are starving,—you are starving, and I am starving,—and all day long I tramp these cursed streets, but gain nothing. So it will go on, day in, day out. Not only we ourselves, but our son too must die. We must save him."

" Yes," said Xantippe, quietly, repeating her husband's words as she kissed the forehead of her child, " we must save him."

" There is only one way."

" Only one way," repeated Xantippe, dreamily. There was a pause, and then, as though the words had grown to have a meaning to her that she could not fathom, she queried, " What way, Gregorio? "

" That," he said, roughly, as he caught her by the wrist, and, dragging her to the window, pointed to the women in the street beneath.

Xantippe hid her face on her husband's breast and cried softly, while she murmured, " No, no; I will never consent."

"Then the child will die," answered the Greek, curtly, flinging her from him.

And the poor woman cast herself upon the bed beside her boy, and when her tears ceased for a moment stammered, "When?"

"To-morrow," was the answer, cruel and peremptory. And as Gregorio closed the lattice, shutting out the noise of song and laughter, the room echoed with the mighty sobbing of a woman who was betrayed, and who repeated hysterically, while kissing the face of her child, "To-morrow, to-morrow there will be food for you."

And Gregorio slept peacefully, for the danger of starvation was over; he would yet live to see his son become rich.

And the woman?

He kissed her before he slept, and women always cry.

IV

CONCERNING TWO WOMEN

GREGORIO felt a little bit ashamed of himself next morning. The excitement had passed, and the full meaning of his words came back to him and made him shudder. The sun, already risen, sent shafts of light between the lips of the wooden lattice. A faint sound of life and movement stole upward from the street below. But Xantippe and the boy still slumbered, though the woman's form shook convulsively at times, for she sobbed in her sleep.

Gregorio looked at the two for a minute and then raised himself with an oath. The woman's heavy breathing irritated him, for, after all, he argued, it was her duty as well as his to sacrifice herself for the lad. Moreover, the Jew must be paid, and to-day was that appointed by Amos for the settling of their account. There was no money to pay it with, and they must lose their furniture, so much at least was certain. But Amos would not have the best of the bargain, thought the Greek as he looked round the room with a grin, and the certainty that he had got the better of Amos for the moment cheered his spirits. Then, too, after to-day there would be plenty to eat, for his wife could manage to earn money; nor was the man so mean in his villainy as to shirk any effort to earn money himself. After first looking at his wife critically and with a satisfied smile, he touched her on the shoulder to wake her.

" I am going out for work," he said, as Xantippe opened her eyes.

" All right."

" Good-bye."

But Xantippe answered not. She turned her face to the wall wearily as Gregorio left her.

Entering the street he made straight for Amos's house, and told the porter, who was still lying on the trestle before the door, that he could not pay

the Jew's bill.   Then, without waiting for an answer, he hurried off to the quay.

With better luck than on the previous day, he
managed to obtain employment for some hours.
The Greek mail-boat had arrived, and under the
blazing sun he toiled good-humouredly and patiently.   The work was hard, but it gave him no
opportunity of thinking.   He had to be continually dodging large bales of fruit and wine, and if
he made a mistake the officer on duty would shout
at him angrily, " Lazy dog! you would not have
left Greece were you not an idle fellow."   Such
words wounded his pride, and he determined to do
so well that he should earn praise.   But the little
officer, his bright buttons flashing in the sunlight,
who smoked quietly in the intervals of silence,
never praised anybody; but he left off abusing
Gregorio at last, and when work ceased for the
day bade him come again on the morrow.

At sunset Gregorio pocketed his few hard-earned
piastres and wandered cityward.   He did not care
to go back to his home, for he knew there would
be miserable stories to tell of the Jew's anger, and,
moreover, he was terribly thirsty.   So he went into
a little café—known as the Penny-farthing Shop—
opposite his house and called for a flask of kephisa.
As he sipped the wine he glanced up nervously at
his window and wondered whether his wife had already left home.   Were he sure that she had, he
would leave his wine untouched and hasten to look
after his son and give him food.   But until he knew

Xantippe had gone he would not move. The sobs of yesterday still disturbed him, and he was more than once on the point of cancelling his resolves. But as the wine stirred his blood he became satisfied with what he had done and said. The little café at Benhur that was to make his fortune seemed nearly in his grasp. It was absurd, he argued, to worry over trifles. Had he not, he asked himself, worked all day without a murmur? It was right Xantippe should help him.

As he sat dreamily thinking over these things, and watching the shadows turn to a darker purple under the oil-lamps, a woman spoke to him.

" Well, Gregorio, are you asleep? "

" No," said he, turning toward his questioner.

The woman laughed. She was a big woman, dressed in loose folds of red and blue. Her hair was dishevelled, and ornamented with brass pins fastened into it at random. Her sleeves were rolled up to her armpits, and she had her arms akimbo—fat, flabby arms that shook as she laughed. Her eyes were almost hidden, she screwed them up so closely, but her wide mouth opened and disclosed a row of gigantic, flawless teeth.

Gregorio frowned as he looked at her. He knew her well and had never liked her. But he dare not quarrel with her, for he owed her money, and " for the love of his black eyes," as she told him, she had ever a bottle of wine ready for him when he wished.

"Well, my good woman," he blurted out, surlily, "you seem to be amused."

"I am, Gregorio. Tell me," she continued, slyly, seating herself beside him and placing her elbows on the table, "how is she?"

"Who?"

"Xantippe. She came to me to-day, and I saw she had been crying. But I said nothing, because it is not always wise to ask questions. I thought she wept because she was hungry and because the baby was hungry. I offered her food and she took some, but so little, scarcely enough to cover a ten-piastre piece. 'That is for the baby,' I said; 'now some for you.' But she refused."

"Perhaps she had food for herself," said Gregorio, shifting uneasily in his chair.

"Perhaps," said the woman, and laughed again, more loudly than ever, till the table shook. "But she asked me for something else," she continued, when her merriment languished for want of breath; "she asked me to let her have an old dress of mine, a bright yellow-and-red dress, and she borrowed some ornaments. It is not right of you, Gregorio, to keep an old friend on the door-step when you have a fantasia."

Gregorio scowled savagely. After a pause he said, "I don't know why my wife wanted your dress and ornaments."

"Oh yes, you do, friend Gregorio." And she laughed again, this time a suppressed, chuckling laugh that threatened to choke her; and she supported her chin on her hands, while her eyes peered through the enveloping fat at the man who sat opposite to her. Suddenly she stood up, and taking Gregorio by the arm dragged him to the door.

" See, there she goes. My garments are cleverly altered and suit her finely, don't they? Ah, well, my friend, a man who cannot support a wife should marry a woman who can support him."

Gregorio did not stop to answer her, but pushed past her into the street. The woman watched him enter the house opposite, and then returned quietly to her work. But there was a smile hovering round her lips as she murmured to herself, " Ah, well, in time."

Gregorio meanwhile had run up to his room and entered it breathless with excitement. The first glance told him that Amos had seized all he could, for nothing remained save a wooden bench and one or two coarse, half-disabled cooking utensils.

Gregorio swore a little as he realised what had happened. Then he saw in a corner by the window his son and Ahmed.

" She has gone," said Ahmed, as Gregorio's gaze rested on him. But she might have gone merely to market, or to see a neighbour, for all the imperturbable Arab face disclosed. As soon as he had spoken the man bent over the child, laughing softly as the youngster played with his beard. For the Arab, as he is miscalled, is fond of children, and there are none to whom children take so readily as to the Egyptian fellahin.

Gregorio watched the two for a moment, and then placing his remaining piastres in the man's hand bade him bring food and wine. As soon as he was left alone with his son, he flung himself down on the floor and kissed the child passionately, half singing to himself, "You shall be a great man, ay, a rich man, my son."

He repeated the sentence over and over again, punctuating it with kisses, while the two-year-old regarded him wonderingly, until Ahmed returned.

When the meal was ended Gregorio took the boy in his arms and sang to him softly till at last the infant slept. Then he placed him gently on the floor, having first made of his coat a bed, and went to the window and flung back the shutters. He smoked quietly as the minutes went by, waiting impatiently for his wife to return. It seemed to him monstrous that the boy who was to inherit a fortune should be sleeping on the dirty floor wrapped in an old coat; that an Arab, a mere fellah, should amuse his son and play with him, when Greek nurses were to be hired in Alexandria had one only the money. Long after midnight he heard a step on the stairs, and a minute after the door opened. He recognised his wife's footsteps, and he rose to meet her. As she came into the room she looked quickly round, and seeing her son went toward him and kissed him. Gregorio, half afraid, stood by the window watching her. She let her glance rest on him a minute, then she turned round and laid her cloak upon the floor.

" Xantippe!"

But she did not answer.

"Xantippe, I have fed our son. The good days are coming when we shall be rich and happy."

But Xantippe was too busy folding out the creases of her cloak to notice him. The moonlight streamed on to her, and her face shone like an angel's. Gregorio made one step toward her, ravished, for she had never appeared so beautiful to him. For the moment he forgot the whole hideous history of the last few days and the brief, horrible conversation of the night before. Fired with a desire to touch her, to kiss her, to whisper into her ear, in the soft Greek speech, all the endearments and tendernesses that had won her when he wooed her, he placed his hand upon her arm. As if stung by a venomous snake, the woman recoiled from his touch. With a quick movement she sprang back and flung at his face a handful of gold and silver coins.

"Take them ; they 're yours," she cried, huskily, and retreated into the farthest corner of the room.

With a savage curse Gregorio put his hand to his lips and wiped away the blood, for a heavy coin had cut him. Then he ran swiftly downstairs, and Xantippe, as she lay down wearily beside her boy, heard a woman laugh.

V

XANTIPPE LOOKS OUT OF THE WINDOW

THE Penny-farthing Shop was full of customers,
and Madam Marx, the fat woman who followed
Gregorio to the bar, was for a long time busy at-
tending to her clients.   Some English war-ships
had entered the harbour at sunset, and many of
the sailors had lost no time in seeking out their
favourite haunt.   Most of them knew Madam
Marx well, as a good-natured woman who gave
them plenty to drink for their money, and secreted
them from the eyes of the police when the liquor
overpowered them.   Consequently there was much
laughter and shaking of hands, and many a rough
jest, which Madam Marx responded to in broken
English.   Gregorio watched the sailors gloomily.
He hated the English, for even their sailors seemed
to have plenty of money, and he recalled the rich
Englishman he had seen at the Café Paradiso,
drinking champagne and buying flowers for the
Hungarian woman who played the fiddle.   The
scene he had just left contrasted disagreeably with
the fun and jollity that surrounded him.   But he
felt unable to shake off his gloom and annoyance,
and Madam Marx's attentions irritated him.   He
felt that her eyes continually rested on him, that,
however busy she might be, he was never out of
her thoughts.   Every few minutes she would come

toward him with a bottle of wine and fill up his glass, saying, "Come, my friend; wine is good and will drown your troubles." And though he resented her patronage, knowing he could not pay, he nevertheless drank steadily.

Every few minutes he heard the sound of horses' hoofs on the hard roadway, and through the windows he saw the military police pass slowly on their rounds.

At last the strong drinks so amiably retailed by Madam Marx did their work, and the men lay about the floor asleep and breathing heavily. The silence succeeding the noise startled Gregorio from his sullen humour. Madam Marx came and sat beside him, weary as she was with her long labours, and talked volubly. The wine had mounted to his head, and he answered her in rapid sentences, accompanying his words with gesture and grimace. What he talked about he scarcely knew, but the woman laughed, and he took an insane delight in hearing her. Just before daylight he fell asleep, resting his head on his arms, that were spread across the table. Madam Marx kissed him as he slept, murmuring to herself contentedly, "Ah, well, in time."

When Gregorio woke the sun was high in the heavens, blazing out of a brazen sky. Clouds of dust swept past the door from time to time, and cut his neck and face as he stood on the threshold smoking lazily. It was too late to go down to the quay, for his place must have long ago been filled

by another. He was not sorry, since he by no
means desired to toil again under the hot sun ; the
heavy drinking of the night had made him lethar-
gic, and he was so thirsty the heat nearly choked
him. He called out to a water-carrier staggering
along in the scanty shade on the opposite side of
the street, and took eagerly a draught of water.
He touched the pigskin with his hand, and it was
hot. The water was warm and made him sick ;
he spat it from his mouth hastily, and hearing a
laugh behind him, turned round and saw Madam
Marx.

"See, here is some wine, my friend; leave the
water for the Arabs."

Gregorio gratefully seized the flagon and let
the wine trickle down his throat, while Madam
Marx, with arms akimbo, stood patiently before
him.

"I must go now," he said, as he handed back
the half-emptied flask.

" Why? "

" Because I must get some work."

" It is not easy to get work in the summer."

" I know, but I must get some. I owe money
to Amos."

" Yes, I know. But your wife is making money
now."

The man scowled at her. " How do you know
that? Before God, I swear that she is not."

" Come, come, Gregorio. You were drunk last
night, and your tongue wagged pretty freely. It 's

not a bit of use being angry with me, because I
only know what you 've told me. Besides, I 'm
your friend, you know that."

Gregorio flushed angrily at the woman's words,
but he knew quite well it was no use replying to
them, for she was speaking only the truth. But
the knowledge that he had betrayed his secret annoyed him. He had grown used to the facts and
could look at them easily enough, but he had not
reckoned on others also learning them.

He determined to go out and find work, or at
any rate to tramp the streets pretending to look
for something to do. The woman became intolerable to him, and the Penny-farthing Shop, reeking
with the odour of stale tobacco and spilled liquor,
poisoned him. He took up his hat brusquely and
stepped into the street.

Madam Marx, standing at the door, laughed at
him as she called out, " Good-bye, Gregorio ; when
will you come back? "

He did not answer, but the sound of her laughter
followed him up the street, and he kicked angrily
at the stones in his path.

At last he passed by the Ras-el-Tin barracks.
He looked curiously at the English soldiers. Some
were playing polo on the hard brown space to the
left, and from the windows of the building men
leaned out, their shirt-sleeves rolled up and their
strong arms bared to the sun. They smoked short
clay pipes, and innumerable little blue spiral clouds
mounted skyward. Obviously the heat did not

greatly inconvenience them, for they laughed and
sang and drank oceans of beer.

The sight of them annoyed Gregorio. He
looked at the pewter mugs shining in the sunlight.
He eyed greedily the passage of one from hand
to hand; and when one man, after taking a long
pull, laughed and held it upside down to show him
it was empty, he burst into an uncontrollable fit of
anger, and shook his fist impotently at the soldiers,
who chaffed him good-naturedly. As he went
along by the stables, a friendly lancer, pitying him,
probably, too, wearying of his own lonely watch,
called to him, and offered him a drink out of a
stone bottle. Gregorio drank again feverishly, and
handed the bottle back to its owner with a grin,
and passed on without a word. The soldier
watched him curiously, but said nothing.

When he reached the lighthouse Gregorio flung
himself on to the pebble-strewn sand and looked
across the bay. The blue water, calm and unruffled
as a sheet of glass, spread before him. The ships
—Austrian Lloyd mail-boats, P. and O. liners, and
grimy coal-hulks—lay motionless against the white
side of the jetty.

The khedive's yacht was bright with bunting,
and innumerable fishing-boats near the breakwater
made grateful oases in the glare whereon his eyes
might rest. But he heeded them not. Angrily he
flung lumps of stone and sand into the wavelets
at his feet, and pushed back his hat that his face

might feel the full heat of the sun. Then he lit a cigarette and began to think.

But what was the good of thinking? The thoughts always formed themselves into the same chain and reached the same conclusion; and ever on the glassy surface of the Levantine sea a woman poised herself and laughed at him.

When the sun fell behind the horizon, and the breakwater, after dashing up one flash of gold, became a blue blur, Gregorio rose to go. As he walked back toward the Penny-farthing Shop he felt angry and unsatisfied. The whole day was wasted. He had done nothing to relieve his wife, nothing to pay off Amos. Madam met him at the door, a flask of wine in her hand. Against his will Gregorio entered her café and smiled, but his smile was sour and malevolent.

"You want cheering, my friend," said madam, laughing.

"I have found nothing to do," said Gregorio.

"Ah! I told you it would be hard. There are no tourists in Alexandria now. And it is foolish of you to tramp the streets looking for work that you will never find, when you have everything you can want here."

"Except money, and that's everything," put in Gregorio, bluntly.

"Even money, my friend. I have enough for two."

Madam Marx had played her trump card, and

she watched anxiously the effect of her words. For a moment the man did not speak, but trifled with his cigarette tobacco, rolling it gently between his brown fingers. Then he said :

"You know I am in debt now, and I want to pay off all I owe, and leave here."

"Yes, that 's true, but you won't pay off your debts by tramping the streets, and your little café at Benhur will be a long time building, I fancy. Meanwhile there is money to be made at the Penny-farthing Shop."

"What are your terms?" asked Gregorio, roughly.

The woman laughed, but did not answer. The stars were shining, and the kempsin that had blown all day was dead. It was cool sitting outside the door of the café under the little awning, and pleasant to watch the blue cigarette smoke float upward in the still air. Gregorio sat for a while silent, and the woman came and stood by him. "You know my terms," she whispered, and Gregorio smiled, took her hand, and kissed her. At that moment the blind of the opposite house was flung back. Xantippe leaned out of the window and saw them.

VI

BABY AND JEW

WHEN the Penny-farthing Shop began to fill Gregorio disappeared quietly by the back door. He muttered a half-unintelligible answer to the men who were playing cards in the dim parlour through which he had to pass, who called to him to join them. Gaining the street, he wandered along till he reached the bazaars, intending to waste an hour or two until Xantippe should have left the house. Then he determined to go back and see the boy in whom all his hopes and ambitions were centred, who was the unconscious cause of his villainy and degradation.

There was a large crowd in the bazaars, for a Moolid was being celebrated. Jugglers, snakecharmers, mountebanks, gipsies, and dancing-girls attracted hundreds of spectators.

The old men sat in the shadows of their stalls, smoking and drinking coffee. They smiled gravely at the younger people, who jostled one another good-humouredly, laughing, singing, quarrelling like children. Across the roadway hung lamps of coloured glass and tiny red flags stamped with a white crescent and a star. Torches blazed at intervals, casting a flickering glow on the excited faces of the crowd.

Gregorio watched without much interest. He had seen a great many fantasias since he came to Egypt, and they were no longer a novelty to him. He was annoyed that a race of people whom he despised should be so merry when he himself had so many troubles to worry him. He would have liked to go into one of the booths where the girls danced, but he had no money, and he cursed at his stupidity in not asking the Marx woman for

some.   He no longer felt ashamed of himself, for
he argued that he was the victim of circumstances.
Still he wished Xantippe had not looked out of the
window, though of course he could easily explain
things to her.   And Xantippe was really so angry
the night before, explanations were better post-
poned for a time.   "After all, " he thought," it really
does not much matter.   Once we get over our
present difficulties we shall forget all we have gone
through."   This comfortable reflection had been
doing duty pretty often the last day or two, and
though Gregorio did not believe it a bit, he always felt it was a satisfactory conclusion, and one
to be encouraged.

Meanwhile he would not meet Xantippe.   That
was a point upon which he had definitely made up
his mind.   As he strolled through the bazaars,
putting into order his vagabond thoughts, in a tall
figure a few yards in front of him he recognised
Amos.   Nervous, he halted, for he had no desire
to be interviewed by the Jew, and yet no way of
escape seemed possible.

Nodding affably to the proprietor, he sat down
on the floor of a shop hard by and watched Amos.
The old man was evidently interested, for he was
laughing pleasantly, and bending down to look at
something on the ground.   What it was Gregorio
could not see.   A knot of people, also laughing,
surrounded the Jew.   Gregorio was curious to see
what attracted them, but fearful of being recognised by the old man.   However, after a few mo-

ments his impatience mastered him, and he stepped up to the group.

" What is it? " he asked one of the bystanders. " Only a baby. It 's lost, I think."

Gregorio pushed his way into the centre of the crowd and suddenly became white as death.

There, seated on the ground, was his own child, laughing and talking to himself in a queer mixture of Greek and Arabic. Amos was bending kindly over the youngster, giving him cakes and sweets, and making inquiries as to the parents.

A chill fear seized on Gregorio's heart. He could not have explained the cause, nor did he stay and try to explain it. Quickly he broke into the midst of the circle and, catching up the boy in his arms, ran swiftly away.

Having reached home, he kissed the boy passionately, sent for food to Madam Marx, and wept and laughed hysterically for an hour. After a time the boy slept, and Gregorio then paced up and down the room, smoking, and puffing great clouds of smoke from his mouth, trying to calm himself. But he could not throw off his excitement. He imagined the awful home-coming had he not been to the bazaar, and he wondered what he would have done then. A great joy possessed him to see his son safe, and a fierce desire filled him to know who had taken the child away. He longed for Xantippe's return that he might tell her. He forgot completely that he had dreaded seeing her earlier in the evening. Then he began to wonder what Amos was doing at the fantasia, and why he was so interested in the boy. Perhaps Amos would forgive the debt for love of the child. The idea pleased him, but he soon came to understand that it was untenable. Oftener, indeed, he shuddered as he recalled the old man's figure bent over the infant. A sense of danger to come overwhelmed him. In some way he felt that the old man and the child were to be brought together to work his, Gregorio's, ruin.

Suddenly he heard a footstep on the stairs. "Thank God!" he cried, as he ran to the door.

"Xantippe!"

But he recoiled as if shot, for as the door opened Amos entered. The Jew bowed politely to the Greek, but there was an unpleasant twinkle in his eyes as he spoke.

"You cannot offer me a seat, my friend, so I will stand. We have met already this evening."

Gregorio did not answer, but placed himself between the Jew and the child.

"I dare say you did not see me," the old man continued, quietly, "for you seemed excited. I suppose the child is yours. It was surely careless to let him stray so far from home."

"The child is mine."

"Ah, well, it is a happy chance that you recovered him so easily. And now to business."

"I am listening."

"I have already, as of course you know, been here to see you about the money you owe me. I was sorry you did not see fit to pay me, because I had to sell your furniture, and it was not worth much."

"I have no money to pay you, or I would have paid you long ago. I told you when I went to your house that I could not pay you."

"And yet, my friend, it is only fair that a man who borrows money should be prepared to pay it back."

"I could pay you back if you gave me time. But you have no heart, you Jews. What do you care if we starve, so long as—"

"Hush!" said Amos, gravely; "I have dealt fairly by you. But I will let you go free on one condition."

"And that is?"

"That you give me the child."

Gregorio stood speechless with horror and rage at the window, and the old man walked across the room to where the infant lay.

"I have no young son, Gregorio Livadas, and I will take yours. Not only will I forgive you the debt, but I will give you money. I want the child."

"By God, you shall not touch him!" cried Gregorio, suddenly finding voice for his passion.

He rushed furiously at Amos, gripped him by the throat, and flung him to the far side of the room. Then he stood by his child with his arms folded on his breast, his eyes flashing and his nostrils dilated. Amos quickly recovered himself, and, in a voice that scarcely trembled, again demanded his money.

"Go away," shouted Gregorio; "if you come here again, I will kill you. Twice now have I saved my boy from falling into your hands."

"I wish only to do you a service. You are a beggar, and I am rich enough, thank Heaven, to look after the child. Why should you abuse me because I offer to release you from your debts if you will let me take the child?"

Gregorio answered brusquely that the Jew should not touch the boy. "I will not have him made a Jew."

"Then you will pay me."

"I will not. I cannot."

"I shall take measures, my friend, to force you to pay me. I have not dealt harshly with you. I came here to help you, and you have insulted me and beaten me."

"Because you are a dog of a Jew, and you have tried to steal my son."

A nasty look came into the Jew's eyes,—a cold, cunning look,—and he was about to reply when the door opened and Xantippe entered. She was well dressed, and wore some ornaments of gold. Amos turned toward her, asking the man:

"This is your wife?"

But Gregorio told Xantippe rapidly the history of his adventures with the boy; and the woman, hearing them, moved quietly to the corner where he slept, and took him in her arms.

The Jew smiled. "I see," he said, "that madam has money. She has taken the advice I gave you the other day. Now I know that you can pay me, and if you do not within two days, Gregorio Livadas, you will repent the insults you have heaped on my head this night."

He walked quietly to the corner of the room, where Xantippe sat nursing the boy, touched the child gently on the forehead with his lips, and then went out.

For some minutes neither Xantippe nor Gregorio spoke, but the man rubbed the infant's forehead with his finger as if to wipe out the stain of the Jew's kiss.

VII

XANTIPPE SPEAKS OUT

AT last the silence, roused only by the strident buzzing of the mosquitos, became unendurable. Gregorio gave a preparatory cough and opened his lips to speak, but the words refused to be born. He was unnerved. The odious visitor, the weary-ing day, the memory of Xantippe's face at the window, combined to make him fearful. He watched, under his half-closed lids, his wife crouching on the far side of the boy. Once or twice, as he was rubbing the youngster's forehead, his fingers touched those of his wife as she waved off the mosquitos; but at each contact with them he shivered and his fears increased. He

tried, vainly, to get his thoughts straight, and lit
a cigarette with apparent calmness, swaggering to
the window; but his legs did not cease to trem-
ble, and the unsteadiness of his gait caused Xantippe to smile as she watched him. Resting by
the window, Gregorio widened the lips of the lattice and let in a stream of moonbeams that rested
on wife and child, illumining the dark corner.

" Gregorio!"

" Yes."

" Have you told me all? Is there nothing else
to tell me about our son and the Jew?"

Gregorio felt he must now speak; it was not possible to keep silence longer. He was pleased that
his wife had begun the conversation, for it seemed
easier to answer questions than to frame them.
" I have told you the whole story. There is no
more to tell. It was by accident I found him in
the bazaar, and that devil Amos was bending over
him. I could kill that man."

" What good would that do?"

" Fancy if we had lost the boy! Think of the
sacrifices we have made for him, and they would
have been useless."

" Have you made any sacrifices, Gregorio?"

The question was quietly asked, but there was a
ring of irony in the sound of the voice, and Gregorio, to shun his wife's gaze, moved into the
friendly shadows. For some minutes he did not
answer. At length, with a nervous laugh, he replied:

"Of course. We have both made sacrifices, great sacrifices."

"It is odd," pursued Xantippe, gently, as if speaking to herself, "that you should so flatter yourself. You professed to care for me once; you only regard me now as a slave to earn money for you."

"It is for our son's sake."

"Is it for our son's sake also that you sit with Madam Marx, that you drink her wine, that you kiss her?"

Gregorio could not answer. He felt it were useless to try and explain, though the reason seemed to him clear enough.

"I am glad to have this chance," continued Xantippe, "of talking to you, for we may now understand each other. I have made the greatest sacrifice, and because it was for our son's sake I forgave you. I wept, but, as I wept, I said, 'It is hell for Gregorio too.' But when I looked from the window this afternoon I knew it was not hell for you. I knew you did not care what became of me. It was pleasant for you to send me away to make money while you drank and kissed at the Penny-farthing Shop. I came suddenly to know that the man had spoken truth."

"What man?" asked Gregorio, huskily.

"The man! The man you bade me find. Because money is not gathered from the pavements. You know that, and you sent me out to get money. When I first came back to you I flung the gold at

you; it burned my fingers, and your eagerness for
it stung. But I did not quite hate you, though his
words had begun to chime in my ears: 'In my
country such a husband would be horsewhipped.'
When you were kind I was little more than a dog
you liked to pet. I thought that was how all
women were treated. I know differently now.
You will earn money through me, for it is my
duty to my son, but you have earned something
else."

"Yes?" queried Gregorio.

"My hate. Surely you are not surprised? I
have learned what love is these last few days, have
learned what a real man is like. I know you to
be what he called you, a cur and a coward. I
should never have learned this but for you, and I
am grateful, very grateful. It is useless to swear
and to threaten me with your fists. You dare not
strike me, because, were you to injure me, you
would lose your money. You have tried to degrade me, and you have failed. I am happier
than I have ever been, and far, far wiser. When
a woman learns what a man's love is, she becomes
wiser in a day than if she had studied books for a
hundred years."

Xantippe ceased speaking and, taking her son in
her arms, closed her eyes and fell asleep quietly, a
gentle smile hovering round her lips.

Gregorio scowled at her savagely, and would
have liked to strike her, to beat out his passion
on her white breast and shoulders. But she had

spoken only the truth when she said he dare not touch her. With impotent oaths he sought to let off the anger that boiled in him. He feared to think, and every word she had uttered made him think in spite of himself. The events of sixty hours had destroyed what little of good there was in the man. Save only the idolatrous love for his child, he scarcely retained one ennobling quality.

Little by little his anger cooled, his shame died out of him, and he began to wonder curiously what manner of man this was whose words had so stirred his wife. Wondering he fell asleep, nor did he awaken till the sun was risen.

While eating his breakfast he inquired cunningly concerning this wise teacher of the gospels of love and hate, but Xantippe for a time did not answer.

" Is he a Greek? "

" No."

" A Frenchman? "

" No."

" A German? "

" No."

Suddenly Gregorio felt a kind of cramp at his heart, and he had to pause before he put the next question. He could scarcely explain why he hesitated, but he called to mind the Paradiso café and the red-faced Englishman. He was ready enough to sacrifice his wife if by so doing money might be gained, but he felt somehow hurt in his vanity at the idea of this ugly, slow-witted Northerner usurping his place. With an effort, however, he put the question:

"Is he an Englishman?"

"Yes."

He was seized with a tumult of anger. He spoke volubly, talking of the ignorance of the English, their brutality, their dull brains, their stupid pride. Xantippe waited till he had finished speaking and then replied quietly:

"It cannot matter to you. It is my concern. You have lost all rights to be angry with me or those connected with me."

Gregorio refused to hear reason, and explained how he begrudged them their wealth and fame. "For these English are a dull people, and we Greeks are greatly superior."

"I do not agree with you," Xantippe replied. "I have learned what a man is since I have known him, and I have learned to hate you. You may have more brains—that I know nothing of, nor do I care. He could not behave as you have behaved, nor have sacrificed me as you have sacrificed me. Some of his money comes to you. You want money. Be satisfied."

Gregorio felt the justice of her words, and he watched her put on her hat and leave the room. A minute later, looking out of the window, he saw her link her arm in that of the Englishman of the Paradiso, and across the street, at the threshold of the Penny-farthing Shop, Madam Marx waved her hand to himself and laughed.

VIII

A DESOLATE HOME-COMING

Toward the evening of a day a fortnight later, Gregorio found himself seated in Madam Marx's café, idly watching the passers-by. He was feeling happier, for that was being amassed which alone could insure happiness to him. Each day some golden pieces were added to the amount saved, and the café at Benhur seemed almost within his grasp. The feeling of security from want acted as a narcotic and soothed him, so that the things which should have troubled him scarcely interested him at all. He was intoxicated with the sight of gold. When he had first seen Xantippe and the Englishman together his anger had been violent; but when at last the futility of his rage became certain, his aggressive passion had softened to a smouldering discontent that hardly worried him, unless he heard some one speak a British name. His prosperity had destroyed the last vestiges of shame and soothed his illogical outbursts of fury. He was contented enough now to sit all day with Madam Marx, and returned to his home in the evening when Xantippe was away. He had spoken to her only once since she had told him she hated him. He had strolled out of the café about midday and entered his room. Xantippe was there, talking to her child, and quietly bade him go away.

"It's my room as well as yours," Gregorio had answered.

"It is my money that pays for it," was the reply.

A long conversation followed, but Xantippe met the man's coarse anger with quiet scorn, and told him that if he stayed she should grow to dislike her son since he was the father.

Gregorio was wise enough to control his anger then. For he knew that if she were really to lose her love for the boy, all his chances, and the boy's chances, of ease and prosperity would be destroyed. It was, of course, ridiculous to imagine she would supply him with money then. That she thoroughly loathed him, and would always loathe him, was very certain. So great, indeed, seemed her contempt for him that it was quite possible she might come to hate his child. So he did not attempt to remain in the room, but as he closed the door after him he waited a moment and listened. He heard her heave a sigh of relief and then say to the little fellow, "How like your father you grow! My God! I almost think I hate you for being so like him." Gregorio shuddered as he ran noiselessly downstairs. He never ventured to speak to her again. He argued himself out of the disquiet into which her words had thrown him. He knew it was difficult for a woman to hate her child. The birth-pains cement a love it requires a harsh wrench to sever. He easily persuaded himself, as he sipped Madam Marx's coffee, that if he kept in the background all cause for hatred would be removed. As for her feelings toward himself, he had ceased, almost, to care. The money was worth the cost paid in the attainment of it, and a woman's laugh was less sweet to him than the chink of gold and silver pieces. On the whole Gregorio had little reason to be troubled; only unreasoning dislike for the Englishman—why could not he be of any other nation, or, if an Englishman, any other Englishman?—hurt his peace of mind. And for the most part his discontent only smouldered.

Madam Marx brought her coffee and sat beside him. Her face betokened satisfaction, and she looked at Gregorio with a possessive smile. She had gained her desire, and asked fortune for no other gift.

"You have not seen Xantippe since she turned you out? Ah, well, it is much better you should keep away. You are welcome here, and it is foolish to go where one is not wanted."

"I 've not seen her; I 'm afraid to see her." He spoke openly to madam now.

"Some women are queer. If she had ever really loved you, she would not have thrown you over. I should not have complained had I been in her place. One cannot always choose one's lot."

"It 's that damned Englishman who has spoiled her."

"Ah, yes, those English! I know them."

"Did I tell you what she said about the boy? "

"Yes, my friend. But as long as you don't worry her, her words need not worry you."

"They don't, except sometimes at night. I wake up and remember them, and then I am afraid."

"Why do you hate the Englishman? To my mind it is lucky for both of you that this Englishman saw her. There are no men so rich as the English, and he is a rich Englishman. You are lucky."

"I hate him."

"Because he has stolen your wife's love?" Madam Marx, as she put the question, laid her fat hand upon Gregorio's shoulder and laughed confidently. The movement irritated him, but he never tried to resist her now.

"No, not quite that. I'm used to it, and the money more than compensates me. But I hated the man when I first saw him in the Paradiso. There was a fiddler-woman he talked to, and he could scarcely make himself understood. He had money, and he gave her champagne and flowers. And I was starving, and the woman was beautiful."

Madam tapped his cheek and smiled.

"The woman can't interest you now. Also you have money—his money."

"Still I hate him."

"You Greeks are like children. Your hatred is unreasonable; there is no cause for it."

"Unreasonable and not to be reasoned away."

"Well, why worry about him? He won't follow you to Benhur, I fancy."

"It does n't worry me generally; but when you mention him my hate springs up again. I forget him when I am by myself."

" Forget him now."

And they drank their coffee in silence.

Darkness came on, and the blue night mist. Gregorio was impatient to see his son. He gazed intently at the door of the opposite house, little heeding madam, who was busy with preparations for the evening's entertainment of her customers. Suddenly he saw a woman leave the house, hail a passing carriage, and drive rapidly down the street toward the Place Mehemet Ali. Gregorio, with a cry of pleasure, rose and left the café. Madam Marx followed him to the door and called a good-night to him. Gregorio stood irresolutely in the middle of the road. He had promised the boy a boat, and he blamed himself for having forgotten to buy it. Grumbling at his forgetfulness, he hurried along the street, determined to waste no time. On occasions he could relinquish his lazy, slouching gait, and he would hurry always to obey the commands of the king his son. A pleasant smile at the thought of the pleasure his present would cause softened the sinister mould of his lips, and he sang softly to himself as he moved quickly cityward.

Before he had gone many yards an oath broke in upon the music, and he darted swiftly under the shadow of a wall; for coming toward him was Amos the Jew. But the old man's sharp eyes detected the victim, and, following Gregorio into his hiding-place, Amos laid his hand upon the Greek.

"Why do you try to hide when we have so much to say to one another?"

Gregorio shook himself from the Jew's touch and professed ignorance of the necessity for speech.

"Come, come, my friend, the money you borrowed is still owing in part."

"But you will be paid. We are saving money; we cannot put by all we earn—we must live."

"I will be paid now; if I am not, you are to blame for the consequences."

And with a courtly salute the Jew passed on. Now Gregorio had not forgotten his debt, nor the Jew's threats, and he fully intended to pay what he owed. But of course it would take time, and the man was too impatient. He realised he had been foolish not to pay something on account; but it hurt him to part with gold. He determined, however, to send Amos something when he returned home. So good a watch had been kept, he never doubted the child's safety. But it would be awkward if Amos got him put in jail. So he reckoned up how much he could afford to pay, and, having bought the toy, returned eagerly home. He ran upstairs, singing a barcarole at the top of his voice, and rushed into the room, waving the model ship above his head. "See here," he cried, "is the ship! I have not forgotten it." But his shout fell to a whisper. The room was empty.

With a heartbroken sob the man fell swooning
on the floor.

IX

A DISCOVERY AND A CONSPIRACY

For long he lay stretched out upon the floor
in a state of half-consciousness. He could hear the
mosquitos buzzing about his face, he could hear,
too, the sounds of life rise up from the street below;
but he was able to move neither arm nor leg, and
his head seemed fastened to the floor by immova-
ble leaden weights. That his son was lost was all
he understood.

How long he lay there he scarcely knew, but it
seemed to him weeks. At last he heard footsteps
on the stairs. He endeavoured vainly to raise himself, and, though he strove to cry out, his tongue
refused to frame the words. Lying there, living
and yet lifeless, he saw the door open and Amos
enter. The old man hesitated a moment, for the
room was dark, while Gregorio, who had easily
recognised his visitor, lay impotent on the floor.
Before Amos could become used to the darkness
the door again opened, and Madam Marx entered
with a lamp in her hand. Amos turned to see who
had followed him, and, in turning, his foot struck
against Gregorio's body. Immediately, the woman
crying softly, both visitors knelt beside the sick
man. A fierce look blazed in Gregorio's eyes, but

the strong words of abuse that hurried through his brain would not be said.

"He is very ill," said Amos; "he has had a stroke of some sort."

"Help me to carry him to my house," sobbed the woman, and she kissed the Greek's quivering lip and pallid brow. Then rising to her feet, she turned savagely on the Jew.

"It is your fault. It is you who have killed him."

"Nay, madam; I had called here for my money, and I had a right to do so. It has been owing for a long time."

"No; you have killed him."

"Indeed, I wished him well. I was willing to forgive the debt if he would let me take the child."

A horrid look of agony passed over Gregorio's face, but he remained silent and motionless. The watchers saw that he understood and that a tempest of wrath and pain surged within the lifeless body. They stooped down and carried him downstairs and across the road to the Penny-farthing Shop. The Jew's touch burned Gregorio like hot embers, but he could not shake himself free. When he was laid on a bed in a room above the bar, through the floor of which rose discordant sounds of revelry, Amos left them. Madam Marx flung herself on the bed beside him and wept.

Two days later Gregorio sat, at sunset, by Madam Marx's side, on the threshold of the café.

He had recovered speech and use of limbs. With wrathful eloquence he had told his companion the history of the terrible night, and now sat weaving plots in his maddened brain.

Replying to his assertion that Amos was responsible, Madam Marx said:

"Don't be too impetuous, Gregorio. Search cunningly before you strike. Maybe your wife knows something."

"My wife! Not she; she is with her Englishman. Amos has stolen the boy, and you know it as well as I do. Did n't he tell you he wanted the child? I met him that night, and he told me if I did not pay I had only myself to blame for the trouble that would fall on me."

"Come, come, Gregorio, cheer up!" said the woman; for the Greek, with head resting on his hands, was sobbing violently.

"I tell you, all I cared for in life is taken from me. But I will have my revenge, that I tell you too."

For a while they sat silent, looking into the street. At last Gregorio spoke:

"My wife has not returned since that night, has she?"

"I have not seen her."

"Well, I must see her; she can leave the Englishman now."

Madam Marx laughed a little, but said nothing.

"There is Ahmed," cried Gregorio, as a blue-clad figure passed on the other side of the street.

He beckoned to the Arab, who came across at his summons.

"You seem troubled," he said, as he looked into the Greek's face; and Gregorio retold the terrible story.

"You know nothing of all this?" he added, suspiciously, as his narrative ended.

"Nothing."

"My God! it is so awful I thought all the world knew of it. You often nursed and played with the boy?"

"Ay, and fed him. We Arabs love children, even Christian children, and I will help you if I can."

"Why should Amos want the boy?" asked Madam Marx, as she put coffee and tobacco before the guests.

"Because I owe him money, and he knew the loss of my son would be the deadliest revenge. He will make my son a Jew, a beastly Jew. By God, he shall not, he shall not!"

"We must find him and save him," said the woman.

"He will never be a Jew. That is not what Amos wants your son for; there are plenty of Jews." Ahmed spoke quietly.

"They sacrifice children," he continued, after a moment's pause; "surely you know that, and if you would save your boy there is not much time to lose."

Gregorio trembled at Ahmed's words. He wondered how he could have forgotten the common report, and his fingers grasped convulsively the handle of his knife.

"Let us go to Amos," he said, speaking the words with difficulty, for he was choking with fear for his son.

"Wait," answered the Arab; "I will come again to-night and bring some friends with me, two men who will be glad to serve you. We Arabs are not sorry to strike at the Jews; we have our own wrongs. Wait here till I come."

"But what will you do?" asked Madam Marx, looking anxiously on the man she loved, though her words were for the Arab.

"Gregorio will ask for his son. If the old man refuses to restore him, or denies that he has taken him, then we know the worst, and then—"

Gregorio's knife-blade glittered in the sunset rays, as he tested its sharpness between thumb and finger. The Arab watched with a smile. "We understand one another," he said. There was no need to finish the description of his plan. With a solemn wave of his hand he left the café.

"That man Ahmed," said Madam Marx, "has a grudge against Amos. It dates from the bombardment, and he has waited all these years to avenge himself. I believe it was the loss of his wife."

"Amos made her a Jewess, eh?" And then, after a pause, Gregorio added:

"So we can depend on Ahmed. To-night I will win back my son or—"

" Or ? " queried madam, tremblingly.

" Or Amos starts on his journey to hell.   God, how my fingers itch to slay him!   The devil, the Jew devil!"

X

AT THE HOUSE OF AMOS

As Ahmed had advised, Gregorio settled himself patiently to await the summons.   Madam would have liked to ask him many questions, and to have extracted a promise from him not to risk his life in any mad enterprise his accomplice might suggest. But though the Greek's body seemed almost lifeless, so quietly and immovably he rested on his chair, there was a restless look in his eyes that told her how fiercely and irrepressibly his anger burned. She knew enough of his race to know that no power on earth could stop him striking for revenge. And she trembled, for she knew also that directly he had begun to strike his madness would increase, and that only sheer physical exhaustion would stay his hand.

Madam Marx was unhappy, and as she waited on her customers her eyes rested continually on the Greek, who heeded her not.   Once she carried some wine to him, and he drank eagerly, spilling a few drops on the floor first.   " It 's like blood," he muttered, and smiled.   Madam hastily covered his mouth with her trembling fingers.

Just before midnight Ahmed arrived with his two
friends. Gregorio saw them at once, and, calling
them to him, they spoke together in low voices for
a few moments. There was little need for words,
and soon, scarcely noticed by the drinkers and
gamblers, they passed out into the street and
walked slowly toward the Jew's house. Ahmed
rapidly repeated the plan of action. When they
reached the door they stood for a moment before
they woke the Arab, and these words passed between them :

" For a wife."

" For a sister."

" For a son."

Gregorio then demanded admittance and led the
way, followed by his three friends. He had visited
the house of Amos before, on less bloody but less
delightful business, and he did not hesitate, but
strode on to where he knew the Jew would be.
His companions stood behind the curtain, awaiting the signal.

Amos looked somewhat surprised at the Greek's
entrance, but motioned him to a seat, and, as on
the occasion of his first visit, clapped his hands
together as a signal that coffee and pipes were
required.

" It is kind of you to come, for doubtless you
wish to pay me what is owing."

" I wish to pay you."

" That is well. I hope you are better again. I
regretted to find you so ill two nights ago."

" I am better."

The conversation ceased, for Gregorio was restless and his fingers itched to do their work.
Something in his manner alarmed Amos, for he
summoned in two of his servants and raised himself slightly, as if the better to avoid an attack.
But he continued to smoke calmly, watching the
Greek under his half-closed lids.

" I have another piece of business to settle with
you."

" Do you want to borrow more money because
I refuse to lend you any? "

" No ; it is you who have borrowed, and I have
come to you to receive back my own."

" I fail to understand you."

Gregorio tried to keep calm, but it was not possible.   Rising to his feet, he bent over the Jew and
cried out :

" Give me back my son, you Jew dog! "

" Your son is not here."

" You lie! by God, you lie!   If he is not here
you have murdered him."

" Madman! " shouted Amos, as the Greek's knife
flashed from its sheath ; but before he or his servants could stay the uplifted arm the Jew sank
back among his cushions, wounded to the heart.
With a shout of triumph and a " Death to all
Jews! " Gregorio turned savagely on the servants
and, reinforced by his companions, soon succeeded
in slaying them.   Then leaving the dead side by
side, the four men dashed through the house seek-

ing fresh victims. Ten minutes later they were in the street again, dripping with the blood of women and men, for in their fury they had killed every human being in the house.

Down the narrow native streets they pushed on quickly, hugging the shadows, toward the Penny-farthing Shop. Madam Marx, her ears sharpened by fear, heard them, admitted them by a side door, and led them quickly to an upper room. Thither she carried water and clean garments, but dared not ask any questions. Sick with anxiety, she re-entered the bar and waited.

At length the murderers appeared and called for coffee, and Madam Marx attended to their wants. In a few minutes the Egyptians left, and Gregorio and she were alone. Coming near him, she placed her hand timidly on his shoulder, and asked him, in a hoarse whisper, to tell her what had happened.

" My son was not there."

" Well? "

" Well, you can guess the rest. Not one person remains alive of that devil's household."

Madam Marx gasped at the magnitude of the crime, and though her terrors increased, her pride in the man capable of so tremendous a revenge increased also.

" What will happen to you? " she found voice to ask.

" Nothing. I must hide here. We were not seen. Besides, you remember the last time a Greek murdered a Jew—it was at Port Said—the

matter was hushed up.   Our consuls care as little
for the Jews as we do.   My God, how glad I am
I killed him!"

His eyes were fixed on the street as he spoke,
and suddenly he started to his feet.   Madam rose
too, and clung to him.   He pushed her roughly
on one side, while an evil smile played on his lips.

"By God, she shall come back now!"

"Who?"

"Xantippe.   There is no need for her to live
with the Englishman now.   Our son is dead and
the Jew in hell.   I will at least have my wife
back."

"She will not come."

"She shall come.   By God, I will make her!   I
have tasted blood to-night, and I am not a child
to be treated with contempt.   I say I will make
her come."

"But if she refuses?"

"Then I will take care she does not go back to
the Englishman."

"You will—" but madam's voice faltered.
Gregorio read her meaning and laughed a yes.

"But, Gregorio, think; you will be hanged for
that.   Your wife is not a Jewess."

But Gregorio laughed again and strode into the
street.   He was mad with grief and the intoxicat-
ing draughts of vengeance he had swallowed.   He
strode across the road and mounted the stairs with
steady feet.   Madam Marx followed him, weeping
and calling on him to come back.   As he reached

the door of his room she flung herself before him, but he pushed her on one side with his feet and shut the door behind him as he entered.

Lying on the threshold, she heard the bolt fastened, and knew the last act of the tragedy was begun.

XI

HUSBAND AND WIFE

As Gregorio entered the room, Xantippe, who was kneeling by a box into which she was placing clothes neatly folded, turned her head and said laughingly:

"You are impatient, my friend; I have nearly—"

But recognising Gregorio, she did not finish the sentence. She sat down on the edge of the box. Her face became white, and the blood left her lips. With a great effort she remained quiet and folded her hands on her lap.

Gregorio looked at her for a moment, a cruel smile making his sinister face appear almost terrible, and his bloodshot eyes glared at her savagely. At last he broke the silence by shouting her name hoarsely, making at the same time a movement toward her. He looked like a wild animal about to spring upon his prey. Xantippe, however, did not flinch, answering softly:

"I am not deaf. What do you want here?"

" It is my room ; I suppose I have a right to be here."

" I apologise for having intruded."

" None of your smooth speeches. The English-man has schooled you carefully, I see. Can you say 'good-bye' in English yet ? "

" Why should I say 'good-bye'? "

" It is time. You will come back to me now."

" Never."

Gregorio laughed hysterically and stood beside her. His fingers played with her hair. In spite of her fear lest she should irritate him, Xantippe shrank from his touch. Gregorio noticed her aversion and said savagely :

" You must get used to me, Xantippe. From to-night we live together again. It is not necessary now for you to earn money."

" I shall not come back to you. I have told you I hate you. It is your own fault that I leave you."

" It will be my fault if you do leave me."

He pushed her on to the mattress and held her there.

" Let us talk," he said.

For a few minutes there was silence, and then he continued :

" Amos is dead, and our debts are paid."

" How did you pay them ? "

" With this," and as he spoke he touched the handle of his knife. " Don't shudder ; he deserved it, and I shall be safe in a few days. These affairs are quickly forgotten. Besides, there is another reason why we should not live as we have lately been living."

Xantippe opened her eyes as she asked, "What reason?"

Gregorio relaxed his hold, for the memory of his loss shook him with sobs. Cat-like, Xantippe had waited her opportunity and sprang away from his grasp. The movement brought the man to his senses. He rushed at her with an oath, waving the knife in his hand. Xantippe prepared to defend herself. They stood, desperate, before each other, neither daring to begin the struggle. Through the awful silence came the sound of sobs and a plaintive voice crying:

"Gregorio, come back, leave her; I love you."

"Is Madam Marx outside?" hissed Xantippe.

"Yes."

"Then go to her. I tell you I hate you." She pointed to the half-filled box—"I was going to leave here to-night. I will never return to you."

"You were going with the Englishman?"

"He is a man."

Gregorio paused a moment, then in a suppressed voice, half choking at the words, said:

"Our son—do you know what has happened to him? You shall not leave me."

"I know about our son. I am glad to think he is away from your evil influence. Let me pass." Xantippe moved toward the door, but Gregorio seized her by the throat.

"You are glad our son is killed; you helped Amos to kill him."

Rage and despair impelled him. Laughing brutally, he struck her on the breast, and, as she tottered, sent his knife deep into her heart. For a few seconds he stood over her exulting, and then opened the door. Madam Marx, white with fear, rushed into the room. Seeing the murdered woman, a look of triumph came into her eyes. But it was a momentary triumph, for she realised at once the gravity of the crime. She had little pity or sorrow to waste on the dead, but she was full of concern for the safety of the murderer.

"This is a bad night's work, Gregorio."

"Is it? She deserved death. I am glad I killed her. God, how peacefully I shall sleep to-night!"

"This is a worse matter than the other, my friend; you must get away from here at once."

"Let us leave the corpse; I am thirsty," Gregorio answered, callously. With a last look at Xantippe dead upon the floor, the two left the room and made fast the bolt before descending the stairs. As they emerged from the doorway into the street, some police rode by, and Gregorio trembled a little as he stood watching them.

"I want a drink; I am trembling," he said, huskily, and followed Madam Marx into the shop.

The sun was beginning to rise, and already signs of a new life were stirring. The day-workers appeared at the windows and in the streets.

"You must get away at night, Gregorio, and keep hidden all day."

"All right. Give me some wine. I can arrange better when my thirst is satisfied."

After drinking deeply he turned and laughed. "It has been a busy time since sunset."

Then, as if a new idea suddenly struck him, he queried cunningly, "There will be a reward offered?"

"I suppose so."

"Then you will be a rich woman."

Madam Marx flung herself at his feet and wept bitterly. The blow was a cruel one indeed. Eagerly she entreated him to retract his words. She reminded him of all she had done for him, of all she would still do. A sort of eloquence came to her as she pleaded her cause, and Gregorio, weary with excitement, kissed her as he asked:

"But why should you not give me up?"

"Because I love you."

Neither blood nor cruelty could stain him in her eyes.

At last her passion spent itself; calmed and soothed by Gregorio's caress she realised again the danger her lover ran. Vainly were plans discussed; no fair chance of escape seemed open. At last Gregorio said:

"I shall leave here to-night for Ramleh and live in the desert for a time. If you help me we can manage easily. When my beard is grown I can get back here safely enough, and the matter will be forgotten. You must collect food and take it by train to the last station, and get the box buried by Ahmed near the palace. I can creep toward it at night unseen."

" But I will come to you at night and bring food and drink."

" No. That would only attract attention. You must not leave your customers. But the drink is the worst part of the matter. I must have water. Get as many ostrich-eggs as you can, and fill them with water, and seal them. Hide these with the food, and I will carry some of them into the farther desert and bury them there."

" Gregorio, if all comes right you will not be sorry you killed her? "

" She hated me. I shall not be sorry."

And Madam Marx smiled and forgot her fears.

XII

IN THE DESERT AND ON THE SEA

By the last train leaving Alexandria for Ramleh, the next evening, Gregorio sought to escape his pursuers. He had heard from Ahmed on the plat-form, just before starting, that Xantippe's body had been discovered, and that already the police were on his track. He sat in a corner of a third-class carriage closely muffled, and eyeing his neighbours suspiciously. He sighed with relief as the train moved out of the station and began to pass by the sand-hills and white villas, showing ghost-like in the damp mist.

When he reached St. Antonio he saw the lights of the casino blazing cheerfully, and the pure clear desert air invigorated him. Fascinated by the glare, he strolled toward the casino and decided, in spite of the risk, to enter. He watched from a corner the players, and greedily coveted the masses of gold and silver piled in pyramids behind the croupiers. He heard the violins playing Suppé's overture, and the remembrance came vividly to him of the Paradiso and the fair girl with whom the Englishman talked. The exciting events following that evening passed before him—a lurid panorama.

An hour fled quickly away; then he sought the solitude of the desert, and, having collected into a bag as much food and as many eggs as he could carry, he walked away over the sands.

Under the stars he dug holes wherein to bury the eggs, and marked the spots with stones; then, wrapping himself in his cloak, lay down to sleep. All next day he loitered idly about, shunning the gaze of every wandering Arab. When evening came he drew near to the palace to seek for food. To his horror, the box had not been refilled. At first he hardly realised how awful was his plight. Then the truth dawned upon him. Ahmed and Madam Marx must have been arrested. He drew near to the casino and stood under the open windows listening. A cold shudder ran down his back, his face grew pale, and his lips trembled, for he heard two men discussing the murder and the capture of his friends. An involuntary smile lighted up the gloom of his features for a moment as one remarked that the chief offender, the woman's husband, had eluded pursuit. Then he crept back into the desert and waited for the dawn.

The sun rose, fiery and relentless, glittering on the waters of Aboukir, and the cloudless heaven blazed like a prairie on fire. At midday, when its rays fell straight upon him, his thirst became intense, and with feverish fingers he dug up an egg. It was empty. He tossed it away and dragged himself to another hole. The second egg was empty. In turn he dug up all his eggs, and all alike were empty. Improperly sealed, scantily covered by the sand, the water had evaporated. A great despair seized him; he called on God in his anguish, and the silence of the desert terrified him. In a fit of desolate anger he pulled off his cap, and summoned all the saints, Christ, and God Himself, to enter it, and then trampled on it, laughing wildly. Then he flung himself upon the sand, his head still left bare to the pitiless sun. He knew the end had come, but there was not any regret in his heart for his crimes, only an impotent dismay and anger at his solitary condition. The thirst increased every minute, and he gripped the sand with his fingers in his agony. His last word was an oath.

At sunset he was dead.

Two days later Madam Marx left Alexandria
by train for Ramleh. There was no evidence
against her, and she had soon been released.
Her own trouble scarcely disconcerted her; she
had feared only for the Greek in the desert. The
thought of his agony, his hunger, goaded her
nearly to madness; but she was a little comforted
when she remembered the eggs. There was
enough water in them to last him two or three
days. It was the hour of sunset when she arrived,
and she instantly set out desertward, carrying a
basket containing wine and food. She had determined to live at the hotel until the days of per-
secution were past. The heavy sand made it hard
to proceed rapidly, but she struggled on bravely,
and when far enough from civilisation called aloud
the signal-word agreed on. But no one answered.
All through the night she wandered, searching, till
within an hour of sunrise; then she gave way and
sat weeping on the sand. With daylight she rose
to her feet, determined to find her lover, but had
scarcely gone twenty yards before, with a low cry
of grief, she knelt beside the body of a dead
man. In the half-eaten, decayed features she
recognised Gregorio and knew she had come too
late. Undeterred by the hideous spectacle, she
kissed him tenderly and lay beside him.

The sun mounted slowly in the heavens.

The living figure lay as lifeless as the dead.
But after a while the woman rose and dug with her
hands a hollow in the sand. She heeded not the

heat, nor the flight of time, and by evening her work was done.

Raising the body in her arms, she carried it to the hollow and laid it gently down, then tearfully shovelled back the sand till it was hidden. So Gregorio found a tomb. Nor did it remain un-consecrated, for beside it Madam Marx knelt and spoke with faltering lips the remnants of the pray-ers she had learned when a child. As she prayed she watched vaguely a steamer disappear behind the horizon.

The khedival mail-boat *Ramses* sped swiftly over the unruffled surface of the sea. At the stern a tall fair Englishman sat looking on the level shores of Egypt and the minarets of Alexandria. With a sad smile he turned to the child who called to him by his name. They were a strange pair, for the boy was dark and foreign-looking, and there was something of cunning in his restless black eyes. The man's large hand rested softly on the raven curls of the youngster as he muttered to himself:

" For her sake I will watch over you, and you shall grow up to be a true man."

So Xantippe's life had not been lived in vain, for she had loved and been loved, and her memory was sweet to her lover. Moreover, Gregorio's dreams of wealth for his son were to find fulfil-ment, and the sand of the desert, maybe, lies lightly on him.